FIRST
TERRITORY

FIRST TERRITORY

A Novel

Richie Swanson

SUNSTONE PRESS

SANTA FE

Sunstone books may be purchased for educational, business, or sales promotional use. For information please write: Special Markets Department, Sunstone Press, P.O. Box 2321, Santa Fe, New Mexico 87504-2321.

Book and Cover design › Vicki Ahl
Body typeface › Constantia
Printed on acid-free paper
∞

Library of Congress Cataloging-in-Publication Data

Swanson, Richie, 1954-
  First territory : a novel / by Richie Swanson.
       pages cm
  ISBN 978-0-86534-950-6 (softcover : alk. paper)
  1. Pioneers--Fiction. 2. Yakama women--Fiction. 3. Yakama Indians--Wars, 1855-1859
--Fiction. 4. Washington Territory--History--Fiction. I. Title.
  PS3619.W36355F57 2013
  813'.6--dc23
                                2013010082

WWW.SUNSTONEPRESS.COM

SUNSTONE PRESS / POST OFFICE BOX 2321 / SANTA FE, NM 87504-2321 /USA
(505) 988-4418 / ORDERS ONLY (800) 243-5644 / FAX (505) 988-1025

1

The Indian who claimed to own the Umatilla ferry was nowhere along the bank, and I wondered out loud if the governor was the kind to bristle at a delay, but Dominique merely nodded at two canoes poking from beneath willows. He smiled a petite grin for a big-shouldered man, his face leathery, brown as if stained by walnut juice, his lips and high-flung pompadour French-looking, his gaze swamp-water dark, savage from wintering and marrying in frozen caribou wilderness, but shrewd too, grim and confident from his British blood and schooling, and cajoling from factoring at Hudson's Bay posts from the Saint Lawrence to Jasper country and finally to Fort Walla Walla. He reached beneath our wagon and pulled a whipsaw from between two long boards, and we sweated like demons, cutting planks from driftwood, and we piled them into the canoes, so the wagon-wheels would not cut through, and I laid a wobbly board in, and he flung it toward the Umatilla's mouth. "No, you cannot lie out here, not to yourself, not to anyone, not about anything, never!" He glanced at the Columbia boiling and thundering three-miles wide, glaring blindingly in the mid-morning heat. "Your lie might take us across the little-piddling Umatilla, but you tell yourself weak is strong, wobbly is solid, your habit will kill someone someday." Dominique scoffed. "The governor might growl, but he's making treaties like a grizzly nipping a sow too early. The army—General Wool—would leave the interior to the Indians for now."

We unloaded the treaty-gifts, lifted the wagon's wheels into the canoes, reloaded, and I rode my bay roan into the Umatilla, and Dominique braced a log against the wagon, pried the front in, jumped on. He leaped the load jackrabbit-like. He took the reins, and I led the oxen swimming and gawking in terror, the wagon knocking and slamming, the canoes splashing and slapping. The wagon stayed high. The oxen came out un-stumbling, and we left the canoes full of planks splintered by the steel wheels. "See?" said Dominique. "A lie is like an Indian. You must be firm sometimes, must hold a pistol to its head, so it does not rob you."

"Plain enough."

"Ever translated at a council before?"

"No."

"You seem too young."

"Well, I told you I was only five when my folks emigrated."

"Who taught you?"

I shrugged to put him off. I yelled to the team, and he whipped them. We rode along the right bank of the Umatilla, and he left his question alone, but then a long-steep pull brought us atop a sun-burnt plain, and he caught me gazing through the white-earth shimmer toward Yakama country, thinking of Lalooh, her pretty-arched cheeks moistened by clouds of cold-air vapor, her sweet-water voice chattering mysteriously over hard-tongued words the night my brother and I had met her. Jake and I had led mounts and pack horses down a quiet-powdery trail and had reached the frozen Yakama River before we had expected, and Lalooh had stood alone in snowshoes on the ice, lurching, her eyes twinkling candle-like, her braids oiled beneath the starlight, the rest of her covered darkly by a buffalo robe. She eyed the snow on the blankets behind our saddles, the frost in Jake's beard, the raw-red flesh of my younger-peachier face. She peered quickly upriver, guessing we had been aiming for the fire-lit lodge ahead, and then she signed with her hands, showing how the snow had caved in the roof of Father's Sidalia's cabin. *Were we the black gown's new carpenter and farmer?*

Jake and I nodded, dismounting, and four braves walked from the bend behind Lalooh, carrying an old gray-haired Indian, bolstering his limbs as he sang in Yakama, his eyes roiling in trance. "Almcotty," said Lalooh, speaking his name, adding a single word in Chinook, the old trade language. *"Plet." Priest.* The braves carried Almcotty past us, and Lalooh and the braves went briskly upriver, trusting their backs to us, Lalooh glancing over her shoulder, a wisp of a smile sparkling, and Jake and I followed, and more braves descended banks, filing numerously behind us—then squaws, then children crying hunger pangs, stepping around steers and milk cows sprawled on the bank, their bones near-poking out their hides—stock starved to death. We passed cows standing where they had died stupefied with hooves frozen in snow, and then we climbed toward the lodge of tule mats, and the Yakama started to chant, and the braves lowered Almcotty. An old squaw took our guns and horses, and we were whisked inside, left alone, pressed against a wall. One hundred Yakama whooped, then two hundred. Almcotty yelled above them all. He ordered the braves in line, the squaws, the children. He waved, and drummers pounded pom-poms, and Almcotty shrieked, leaping high, springing sideways like a deer, and every savage danced, everyone in line, jerking arms and legs, sweating, dropping to the floor, Lalooh in front, Lalooh shuffling all night, Lalooh's braids bouncing lightly, Lalooh lifting her chin like a princess, her stare flaming copper, holding me against the wall, saving me from glancing in terror at Jake.

Finally a dawn breeze fluffed the lodge, and the Indians rushed out. The snow was gone, and horses were foraging, and Lalooh laughed a softly tinkling bell beside me, naming the wind so sudden and warm, "*Chinook*." "*Plet*," she said again, running the two ideas together, her breath washing my cheek warmly, damply, close.

And then Father Sidalia came sloshing up the bank, walking with a shepherd's staff, bending and swaying like a thin-dark reed, his bare feet moving in a frozen crust turning swiftly into gumbo, his dimples rising blissfully as he chanted a primitive Indian rhythm and sang in deep tenor about Christ entering Jerusalem, palms cut and laid at the savior's feet.

"*Chemookdatpas*," Lalooh had said. "Black gown." *She spoke English.*

Only a few words, she had signed, and she had raised her chin my way, and I had felt a new world as large as the valley below, the clouds lifting rapidly, her bronze face waiting eagerly, her copper eyes shining radiantly beside me.

"Did you get to kissing her?" asked Dominique.

"Traded words for a year."

"You Catholic?"

"No, Ma's reverend in Brownsville told us Sidalia had lost his laymen and needed hands, and Jake and I went to see if what people claimed was true—that Kamiakin country's could hold stock all winter."

Dominique drew in his lips as if to whistle, to show the import of knowing Kamiakin and his band. He knew by heart and years what most of us guessed by hearsay, you see. During the late twenties he had given Kamiakin traps, shot, powder, dog sleds, even a beaver's hat with fox tails and cock feathers—all to induce his band to trade furs with Hudson's Bay Company—and all to no consequence. During the thirties he had sold American emigrants flour and tobacco and had directed them south away from the company's beaver country—also to no consequence. The British border had moved up to the forty-ninth parallel in 'forty-six, the Land Donation Act had passed in 'fifty, California had become a state, and gold-and-settlement fever had swept the fur brigades from the Columbia country as cleanly as locomotives would soon whistle buffalo from the plains.

Washington became its own territory in 'fifty-three, and the company offered to sell Dominique cattle and horses to raise. Dominique had declined, had left his son at Fort Walla Walla and had moved with his Babine wife to Oregon City in Willamette Valley. And a week ago his express had arrived at Jake's claim above The Dalles, where I had been hewing fence posts for the boundary: *"Assistant needed to interpret at the largest Indian council ever held west of the Rocky Mountains. If he proves himself able to speak Yakama, the governor will pay five dollars in gold per day."*

And so Dominique and I drove the team steady across the plain, and we called out Indian words, testing mine against his, and when the heat eased toward dusk, Dominique galloped the horses to a soaking lather, riding through salt weed to a hidden sink of cottonwoods, and he tossed sand on my cooking fire and passed me pemmican from the Cree on the Saskatchewan, moist with berries and buffalo juice, and we encamped invisibly, keeping ourselves as silent as the stars above us.

"Allons!" Dominique shook me in the morning, waking me in French as if I were a voyageur or bourgeois. He walked to wagon ruts at the edge of camp, grasses freshly cut for forage—signs of the governor's party—it had left Fort Dalles two days before I had arrived there, and we had been ordered to catch it.

We drove the team past noon, and we pulled up at the rim of a crest, and Old Glory flapped from a wagon in the Walla Walla Valley below, a handful of Dragoons glittering magnificently on mounts around it, white breast-belts shimmering against blue uniforms, gilt buttons and scabbards winking before the gleaming-winding river, an ocean of prairie behind them.

We rode down, and there in the wagon-bed squirmed the first governor of Washington Territory, thumping violently against buckboards, looking hardly five-feet tall, his head oversized like a dwarf's, his legs child-sized, his pants bunched down around his ankles as if he had soiled his drawers. The governor writhed, pulling up a hernia truss, his narrow-brash eyebrows knitted in pain, his beard immaculately trimmed but wrenched from his exertion—I had read about him in newspapers—he had come from blue-blood Pilgrims in Massachusetts—had suffered an old hay-pitching injury, a rupture from boyhood—had graduated first-in-class from West Point—had taken Mexico City with General Scott—had written election pamphlets for President Pierce—so had earned his appointment and had come out here, surveying railroad routes through the highest-snowiest passes of the Rockies and Cascades.

He finished tying his truss, and his orderly lifted him, and he braced himself against sideboards, pushing against a gold-handled cane, looking as lean and muscled as a mink on the prowl. He flashed a regal smile at Dominique, a cordial beam of his enormous eyes at me, and then everyone waited. He swung his body wincing and looked with menace at bare-wooden rails, a little square fence. He looked at Dominique again, and a kind of prayerful silence passed between them. We had arrived at the site of the old Whitman mission, and we could see between the rails the grave markers of the fourteen Americans massacred eight years ago. But all other signs of Reverend and Narcissa Whitmans' industry—the lean-to where they had first sung Protestant hymns to Indians, the fields and garden, grist mill and stock pens, emigrant house, mansion house trimmed in New England green, the medicine closet where two Cayuse chiefs had axed the reverend, the school from which a Cayuse boy had shot Narcissa, the fruit trees where Cayuse had taken Christian women, the kitchen where Cayuse had butchered a man my age, sick with measles—all were gone without a trace.

"Dominique!" said the governor. "Young Eaton! You will make it clear to the Cayuse that if any one of them gets saucy during the council, he will be seized!"

Dominique nodded coolly.

"Yes sir," I said.

The governor wriggled sharply, and his orderly lowered him, and he lay flat again all the way to the treaty grounds.

And after dark he summoned me, and I stood by his wagon as he sat in the bed, leaning against the sideboards, working a sextant, his legs spread wide, a candle flickering on a crate beside him. He slid the index arm, fixed screws and lenses, looked and looked at the stars and a crescent moon, and then he thrust himself sideways and peered through a telescope I had not seen in the dark. He lifted a watch from the crate, then a thermometer, and he jotted notes, his face in the candlelight giant-looking, his eyebrows so painfully squeezed I dared not breathe or swallow. He reached around himself and put each instrument away in its case, and then he slid adroitly across boards, stood before me, moved instantly past, and I was ushered into his tent, and he received me sitting upon a simple army blanket on a wooden bed frame—almanacs, books and portfolios stacked in lantern-light all around him. He looked down at tables and columns of figures, hours of trigonometry awaiting him—coordinates to be ciphered by Greenwich Time, angular distances, refractions, the courses of heavenly bodies.

He looked up as if we were old friends. "Tell me," he said, "did Chief Kamiakin leave last fall to plan a federation to kill all the whites in the Oregon country?"

Lalooh came to mind again, her taps last fall at the cabin door, her hurry as she had led us deep into willows up Ahtanum Creek—Sidalia had fled with us, carrying his satchel of accoutrements. *"Kamiakin has returned," Sidalia had said. "The clouds are gathering upon all hands. The tempest is pent-up and ready to burst."*

I looked at the governor directly. "I never heard," I said.

"Can you remember last September?" said the governor. "If Kamiakin met with Looking Glass and any Cayuse chiefs? With Kahlotus? Peopeomoxmox? If he met with any Rogue or Spokane or coastal chiefs?"

I remembered how softly Lalooh had returned through the willows the next morning, how the yellow leaves had rustled so quietly Jake and I had drawn pistols before her smile had told us Kamiakin had allowed us to stay, at least through the coming winter.

I shook my head no to the governor, and he downed a cup of bourbon, exasperated. "Come on, my boy! My territory embraces eleven degrees of longitude! Six in latitude! God knows how many tongues! How many tribes! Is my question so hard?"

"I remember Kamiakin reciting letters to Father Sidalia, asking you to keep the whites out of his country. I remember Kamiakin roping his own longhorns and digging his own cabbages and turnips from his garden."

"Did the superior of the mission—Sidalia—have a squaw?"

"No sir."

"Did he and the other Catholic priests talk against America?"

"No sir."

"Did they sell Kamiakin extra powder and balls?"

"No sir."

The governor glared me out, tucking in his leg tiredly, stiffly, wearily.

But when the council opened three days later, he leaned from his cane as lithely as a lynx about to lunge, speaking forcibly, and Kamiakin seethed silently, motionlessly, a shadowy hulk seated beneath the council arbor, his face enormous, his nose broad and fleshy, his shoulders thrust backward as if to communicate his displeasure to semicircle after semicircle of surly-faced braves and squaws broiling in the sun on the ground behind him.

Dominique repeated each sentence of the governor's in the dialect of the Nez Perce, the tribe more numerous than all the others combined. One crier shouted his translation in Nez Perce, another in Wallawalla. The governor's Indian agent for the interior—Thomas Jefferson McKalb—recorded the statements, sitting on the last bench beneath the bower, his eyes sulky. The Indians listened. They muttered among themselves. They quieted, and Chief Peopeomoxmox of the Wallawalla rose, his nose as pugnacious-looking as Kamiakin's, his nostrils flaring dismissively at Dominique. "I remember this one from when a Californian shot my son," he said. "This one spoke like an owl coughing rabid mice. He said the white law would hunt and hang my son's killer. He said this many times. But the white law hunted no one but Indians."

Chief Stickus of the Cayuse rose, a silk ascot tied to his buckskin, his small eyes squinting darkly, piercingly. "I have known Dominique Purcell since before Reverend Whitman came, but now I cannot believe his words."

The governor beckoned me. I rose and stood beneath the bower to speak, seeing Lalooh's mother and aunts sitting in the nearest semicircle of squaws, heads alertly raised, hair-parts bare and glistening, braids tight as ropes, shiny as polished musket-barrels. Lalooh was not with them, not behind them, not with any group of squaws, and I had heard nothing of her since Jake and I had left her people.

I repeated Dominique's translation exactly, "The Great Father will not steal his red children's land. He will pay them more than it is worth. He will draw lines, so the whites and the Indians will know what they own. The Great Father will cede his children two reservations, so they can become rich in cattle and farms. The Great Father will give the Yakama, Klickitat and Palus land up the Yakama Valley. He will give the Cayuse, Umatilla and Wallawalla land up the Snake River and in Nez Perce country. His red children will get flour and corn easier to harvest than camas and bitterroot—wooden houses sturdier than lodges—sawmills, gristmills, blacksmith shops—unbreakable axes, shovels, blades and plows. His red women will get a chance to learn to spin and weave and make their own clothes. His red men will someday be doctors, lawyers and farmers just like whites."

"Now we see the governor himself speaks roundabout, tending to evil," said Peopeomoxmox. "We will take no gifts, not a grain of wheat. The Wallawalla want our own land. We Indians here are many bands, many chiefs. We will talk among ourselves and council again with whites at a better time."

The governor raised a handbill: **Gold on the Okanogan! At Kettle Falls! At Colville!** "You have no time to waste," he said. "Miners will come, and you must let them pass. The bad ones will take any squaw found off a reservation. They will steal your children if they find them off reservations."

Dominique and I hid our chagrin behind our smiles, for no one had told us about a strike.

"We will give each chief his own house, gardens, five hundred dollars per year," I translated. "Tell me, what does Kamiakin say? Does he have no heart to help his people?"

"Kamiakin has nothing to say," said Kamiakin.

"Can this be true?" said the governor. "Kamiakin, great chief of the Yakama, does not speak? His people have no voice here today? Is he not afraid?

Ashamed? No? Then speak out!"

I translated, and Kamiakin remained dead-faced. "What have I to speak of?" he said, and he slid his immense-dark gaze to columns of dust billowing suddenly down a low-sloping butte beyond the council grounds—more Cayuse arriving. Warriors painted fantastic colors fanned out, galloped down into Mill Creek, charged splashing up the bank. They raised spears and muskets, clanging shields, singing, circling Dragoons who stood stiffly at attention. The governor in his scarlet neck-scarf and balloon-sleeved blouse walked briskly past the soldiers. He stopped before Blue Hawk waiting high on a stallion, the Cayuse war chief wearing a coyote-head war cap, bear claws dangling, eagle plumes stained vermillion. The governor gestured at kettles of white beef, and Blue Hawk jerked his stallion around, and all the warriors followed, going to eat at Kamiakin's camp, and Dominique counted, noting the number in his red-leather notebook, adding them to his previous count, making nearly two thousand.

And I wrote that evening in the governor's tent, finishing his dispatch to Major Wells at Fort Dalles, *"Three thousand warriors surround us as if to annihilate us, but Kamiakin and all the other chiefs see the wisdom of extinguishing their titles and accepting reservations. Five hundred more troops will keep the hot-blooded young ones cool with fear of our howitzers."*

The orderly announced Lawyer, and we went out, and the Nez Perce chief raised his cheeks high in the long, yellow, evening heat, his raven-hair fluffing thickly to his shoulders, a crucifix hanging against a naked chest puffing proudly—Nez Perce lodges stood around our little treaty camp as thickly as cattle bunched inside a corral, protecting us with thirty times more warriors than the forty-five Dragoons the army had previously allotted us.

A Nez Perce boy dashed between lodges, bringing a little goat of a white man in a cowpoke's clothing—a shirt sleeve tied at the stump of his left arm, a long-tongued quirt strapped there. A second Nez Perce boy appeared with a magnificent strawberry roan, and One-armed Jacobs slung himself into the saddle so instantly and smoothly I wanted to see the feat again, but he was off on his express ride, and I felt pretty thick, knowing what he carried.

"*Itehlecum,*" I said to the governor, telling him I was going to a Yakama bone game. But I made for Kamiakin's camp, not really intending to play. I gambled instead on a stronger urgency, but the sound of a squeezebox slowed my step. Father Sidalia sang in Yakama, a peace song from France, his tenor bellowing as deeply through the evening's heat as it had through the morning's chill the Sunday after the Chinook had melted the snow—Ahtanum Creek had turned into a torrent, holding four and five canoes abreast—the Indians had landed for Easter Feast Day—Sidalia had leaned against his cabin, sinking to shins in mud, singing, playing his squeezebox. Macis the dwarf-girl had greeted the dugouts, dragging her club-foot, pretending to serve communion, tearing bits of bread, and Kamiakin and three braves had carried a freshly killed bear on a pole and had laid the sow at my feet. They had joined the other Yakama sitting on logs and boughs a few rods away, and I had knelt with my knife and considered the bear—the rope Kamiakin had slipped into her den and then around her neck, the withes around her snout, her sheer bulk, and I looked up for Jake, needing buckets, and the bright-eyed squaw peered down, standing soundlessly above me, her pretty cheeks drawn solemnly, a bladder sac in her hand.

"Lalooh," she said, nodding her name. "Almcotty. Kamiakin," she said, signing for the grease. *For their tah, their power. To dream.*

Lalooh knelt beside me, laid a slender finger upon the fur, named the places to cut, her tone grave with her chiefs' authority, her tongue-tip curling with clucks, some sounds too sharp to repeat, others too deep and thick inside her throat. She dressed the bear, naming the parts, and I mangled her words, and she laughed quietly as Sidalia sang, shining her eyes playfully, squeezing grease into the bladder sac, and then she grew very quiet, staring at the ceremony. The dwarf-girl stood before Sidalia, repeating his verses, older than I had thought, her hips just a year younger-looking than Lalooh's, her face flat-nosed but her lips thin, her eyes beaming at Sidalia.

Macis spoke the Ascension in English, turning r's into *acks*, her only mistakes, and Sidalia bowed and handed her a painted stick, a Catholic Ladder, and Lalooh hissed quietly in Chinook. "*Swahale.*" Prayer stick. "Macis *pel'ton.*" Lalooh thought Macis a *fool* for accepting the black robe's Ladder? She disliked Sidalia? All whites?

The creek had stayed high a month, and a day or two after it had dropped inside its banks, Lalooh had busted up through silt-laden willow, raising a team whip, yelling, *"Wah'kpuch!" Rattlesnake.* She had snapped the whip behind Sidalia's cabin, her arm jerked, the whip caught, and another lashed backward, untangling from hers, and I saw Sidalia jerk its handle. He was behind the cabin, and he turned and lashed the ground, and a snake leapt, spraying blood in a pop of dust. The rattler lifted its head. It coiled. It *burred*, and Sidalia drew his whip, and a crack snapped at his hand. His whip-handle flew from him, he grabbed his hand, sucked it, eyed Lalooh disbelieving, and she stepped evenly toward him, raising her whip again, and I could not think in Yakama, though I had been on my way to help Sidalia and Lalooh list words in his Yakama dictionary.

"Whoa!" I yelled in English, *"Kopet'!"* in Chinook. *Stop.*

Lalooh raised her whip higher, and Sidalia lifted his crucifix, thrust it toward her, planted his feet, his robe billowing in the wind as he stiffened. "Here I am, Lalooh! Strike me! Behold my medicine! My *tah!* Christ does not fear! I do not fear!"

"Chemookdatpas pel'ton!" said Lalooh. "Only Almcotty kills *Wah'kpuch!* Only the Indian doctor! No white! No devil robe!"

I ventured toward Lalooh, waving my hat at the snake, "It's gone, Lalooh!"

"Gone?" Sidalia arched a glare toward me, keeping the crucifix aimed at Lalooh. "Would you die in the garden, Andrew? Would you have Jake die?"

"Wah'kpuch knows the bad medicine," said Lalooh. *"Wah'kpuch* will send his men, and they will bite the bad father."

"And then I will know the sweet sound of grace which speaks without a sound," said Sidalia.

His dimples rose, his eyes shone brightly, and Lalooh's whip cracked. The crucifix flew, its chain burst. Sidalia's hair fluffed, barely missed. "Lalooh, Sparkling Water," he said, translating her name. "The good father loves Lalooh." He signed to sprinkle holy water on her head, mine, Jake's, and Lalooh looked at me, lowering her whip, not understanding, and I thought of locust-eyed preachers sweating, speaking heatedly in Illinois, emigrant camps, Brownsville, other towns in Willamette Valley.

Lalooh looked at Sidalia, "Kamiakin told me, yes, I can put Yakama words in your book. But you go against Kamiakin. He told you black robes do not kill

Wah'kpuch."

She walked down into the creek again, mounting her pony, a huckleberry roan waiting on the opposite bank. But she returned the next Sunday—perhaps ordered by Kamiakin—or curious about Young Andrew?

Jake had let Sidalia baptize him. He had taken communion regularly, pretending, hoping to strengthen his place in cattle country. I had not, nor had Kamiakin or Lalooh or most of the other Yakama her age or older. But Lalooh and Macis had attended most of Sidalia's feast days, and so when Agent McKalb had arrived at Ahtanum several weeks ago, each had easily named the Creation, Mary's Assumption, the cross and Eternity pictured on the new Catholic Ladders he had unloaded.

"The governor said I must deliver them myself," Agent McKalb had said, greeting Sidalia. "The Ladders came down the Mississippi by steamboat. They crossed Panama by mule team. They came up the coast by steamship, and I nearly started from Olympia without them. But the governor called me back." McKalb stood admiring the Ladders—he was so tall his head was nearly even with his horse's, his ten-gallon hat was upturned like a stage driver's, his legs and shoulders were strapping-big. His eyes beamed amicably as he grinned, and his mustache—a ruddy auburn—wiggled so minutely it made his face and freckles appear larger than they already loomed. "The governor's having a council in May. He's inviting every chief in the interior, every priest." He handed Lalooh a red ribbon, and she fingered it unsmiling, and he gave one to Macis, and the dwarf-girl tied it to a braid and skip-hopped giggling as we moved toward Sidalia's cabin, McKalb with a bundle of letters for the priest, myself carrying a cask of wine for the mission.

"The governor's going to give chiefs legitimate title to reservations." McKalb ducked through the door, put a little metal box on Sidalia's table, unlocked it, pulled out a government form. "He's ordered me to designate chiefs."

Sidalia lowered a sober glance, and Lalooh and I were off at once—she to fetch Kamiakin, I to hew fence posts. Jake and I were merely working hands that short while ago, you see. We had built and improved cabins for the priests, had put up wood, had made shingles, had ridden after pine resin for incense.

We had branded and herded their stock, and so two days later, while Sidalia had sung his dawn prayers, and McKalb had readied himself to leave, we were out counting horses and cattle, but the stable-gate hung open, and a squaw moaned gibberish inside—Macis lay on a mess of hay, covered only by a government blanket, pig-snot on her legs, blood caked and running down her loins, her breasts bruised and heaving, her breath heavy with sleep-talking, smelling of whiskey, a false-ruby brooch in her fist at her hip.

We had followed the drag of her tracks backward to McKalb's camp and had found no horse, no mule, no tent or agent. "He thinks he gets off early, don't he?" Jake had said, and he had stared for a short while at the empty horizon, resigning himself, knowing Ahtanum had ceased to be a place to secretly dream a ranch.

Sidalia's squeezebox and singing stopped. Pom-poms started. Animal screams and medicine cries came from the Yakama camp, and Sidalia trod swiftly to me, finding me not far from where I had left Lawyer and the governor, just listening, still considering.

"Our Indians might kill us all," said Sidalia, "the governor first."

I looked past him, and he gulped distastefully, snickering, knowing who I sought. "The same light that shone upon Him in the desert can shine upon you here, Young Andrew. Come to the Lord's tent. Let grace forgive your intention."

"Eaton!" The governor, Lawyer and Dominique hurried through the dark, coming from the governor's tent again. "Have you two been visiting your friends on your own?"

"Governor," said Sidalia, "the Indians dislike you. They can pray. They can farm. Given time, they will learn to give glory to this world and the next, but we must dedicate ourselves to teach them well enough."

"What did they say?" said the governor.

"Nothing more than they told you today. You know, God does not love those who deceive. He will punish this council just as He will punish the Indians."

"I await my judgment," said the governor. "I do not doubt."

"We love the black gown," said Lawyer. "We love the governor." He led us past Sidalia and out of the Nez Perce camp and through the Palus camp, and then a brave untied a boundary rope, the Yakama camp, and we squeezed through chanting braves to a ring of dancers, and a scalp flew high, squaws dove as it plummeted, and Lalooh groveled near-naked in the dirt, and she rose screeching, waving the scalp, and she flung it down, stomped it, trampled it, her breasts shaking before me, her braids unloosed like a hag's, ghoulish squares painted around her eyes.

She squatted and leaped again, shrieking, pitching the scalp high, and then she danced toward Kamiakin, and he saw me shrinking, and his stare mocked us, mocked Lawyer too, and the governor glared his disgust, and we left.

The governor pummeled me with questions back at his tent, and I looked at him through a stupor, my mind still reeling from Lalooh's dancing. "My God, why do I pay you, a boy of sixteen?" he said. "Did you know the dervish? Her name? Did she call the scalp a name? A white name?"

"They danced a victory, Kamiakin's boldness," said Dominique. "She is only a squaw, someone's third or fourth woman someday. Do you want her tonight?"

"I want Hudson's Bay posts off American soil and the first transcontinental railroad here in Washington, not in California. I want safe trade from Boston to Puget Sound to Asia."

The governor dismissed us, pulling out old copies of Indian treaties from the east, Cherokee and Chickasaw. He looked for new words to convince Kamiakin, and we climbed into our wagon, and I opened my bedroll, and Dominique handed me rifles, and I loaded and stacked them, a precaution, and the sky rumbled, and the heat got tighter, refusing to cool, and the willow fragrance sharpened inside the canvas, blossoms sugary-sweet, cutting me deeper, making me worse. *How wretchedly Lalooh had flung the scalp. Yet how softly she had rustled through willows last fall.*

The thunder clapped. It retreated. Lightning flashed brightly, faintly, brightly. The storm seemed to stall—like my favor and fancy, you see—my old hunger for Lalooh, the way she had risen on my skin as I had lain gritty in the cabin last spring, knowing Ma would lament if I became a squaw man.

I was a speck of man compared to McKalb, wasn't I? He might have taken

Macis dishonorably, but he had known her only three days, and I had whittled away an entire year, knowing Lalooh, and McKalb had probably had a squaw every chance, visiting tribes during winter and spring, designating chiefs.

Someone's third or fourth woman? Not Lalooh. Dominique hadn't meant it. Dominique mistrusted McKalb, had smiled to himself when the governor had ordered the sulking agent to sit behind us during council, record statements and refrain from visiting chiefs alone anymore.

The wind finally gusted cold. Rain finally slashed down upon the bonnet. I finally slept, and I woke to a crackling-rocky roar, and we scuttled out amid Indians standing everywhere, the creek suddenly high and turbulent, navy-black in the pre-dawn dark, gushing pale-frothing foam across black saplings, the rain finished here, the powdery-gray thunderheads flashing east against the Blue Mountains.

The governor and Lawyer stood eyeing the creek, and Dominique joined them, but Kamiakin was not there, no Yakama was anywhere, and I ducked into willows, heading to their camp, and I came to a little clearing, and Lalooh sat on a bone-white cottonwood log all alone as if in a fairy world, watching the stars as they waned west, seeing the old stories she had told me, the myths of her people.

She smiled warmly, stunning me, her hair freshly clean, her ghoulish squares washed away, and I sat, and she peered down as if modestly or shamefully.

"I have been waiting so long to see you," I said.

"I have been staying beneath my robe every morning, telling my mother I ate something bad," she said. "But I could not pretend tonight."

I took her hand. "The governor pays me gold, and I save almost all of it. When this is finished, I am going to improve a section of cattle land beside your reservation."

"Yes, you're too good a boy to live as a white," she said. "You make the governor postpone this council. Tell him be true, fair to us. Tell him his treaty is bad, and McKalb is bad. Tell him Macis made wedding clothes, and she rode off, looking for him, and she never came back. Tell the governor your Great Father did not make Macis, he did not make our land, they are not his ribbons to give away. Tell him whites can settle along the emigrant road, nowhere else, and when the willow turns yellow again, you come to my father, and I will put up your lodge and dry your fish and tan your hides."

The bugle sounded four o'clock mess, the governor's strict orders, and I got up. "Yes!" I said. "I do! I will!"

And later that morning and every day afterward Lalooh sat in the nearest semicircle of squaws, and I translated not knowing who knew our pledge, or how I could keep it, but the chiefs railed their long-objecting speeches, and I knew their words with sudden ease—so instantly Dominique secretly winked, encouraging me, and the governor reared his beard, holding bated breath, listening through the tribal histories, heathen Creations, claims to spirits in graveyards, crimes of emigrants, murders, bad promises.

On June seventh—our seventeenth evening at the Walla Walla council grounds—Dominique unrolled a map inside the closed and secret heat of the governor's tent, and he traced a third reservation-site south of the Columbia—a concession for the Cayuse, Umatilla and Wallawalla.

Lawyer grunted readily. "Where are your five hundred blue-coats?"

"Denied," said the governor, and he burned a lantern all night, spreading his legs, stretching his old rupture, copying and enlarging the map, correcting lines, detailing springs, drainages, elevations, grazing sites, places where potatoes grew two-pounds, some years even five.

And the next day at the council arbor he held his hand uplifted like a preacher, his voice clapping excitedly, and I translated, "So long as the Columbia runs to the sea shall these three reservations belong to the Indians! So long as the mountains touch the sky, no white man shall live upon them! Lawyer, chief of all Nez Perce, agrees!"

Peopeomoxmox stood with a tomahawk pipe draped around his neck, a British derby shading his gaze, his eyes already dark and resigned. "I would fight Americans until I had no more warriors, but who would take care of my old, my crippled, my children, my women?"

Kahlotus of the Palus rose. Young Chief, Five Crows and Stickus of the Cayuse rose. Each spoke practically like Peopeomoxmox, but Kamiakin remained seated in a green tunic upon a grizzly robe, his massive brow raised delicately, his long hair handsomely wavy, his eyes still refusing.

And then horses approached, and four Nez Perce warriors rode beneath the arbor, three pounding war drums, all singing a war song, their white-haired leader raising a Blackfoot scalp on a pole. "I am Old Looking Glass, war chief!" He thrust a rawhide shield at the governor and glowered at him as if he were a roach in a flour barrel. He swung to his people. "I have been away three years, hunting buffalo, and what have you done? While I have been gone, you have sold the Nez Perce country! Go home to your lodges! I will talk to you!"

I translated the governor's reply, "I have said to every Indian—I say it now—nothing will be done without your consent!"

"You have drawn your own lines, not those of Looking Glass!" said the old war chief.

Peopeomoxmox stepped forward again, "Yes, this is the way of you white people, your chiefs! We shall adjourn the council! Set another time to talk! Many Wallawalla are not here!"

Five Crows spoke, hairs and feathers dangling down his forehead, his French blouse showing the wealth of his horse herds. "We do not want to change the earth and sky around us! We will not leave our old ones beneath the earth! We will not break open our mother!"

Peopeomoxmox glared at Lawyer, "I think you have given away your people's land."

Stickus rose again: "I have been friends with Americans since the Reverend Whitman came. I warned the reverend bad Indians would kill him. I did not hide his killers. I helped find them. But I am troubled by the governor. My people came from Earth. She is our mother. You cannot sell or barter her. You will sicken her, sicken your own people. Suppose you were us, and you came from your mother, and you suckled her, and someone came and took her away?"

Young Chief stepped forward, his lips womanly, his eyes softly almond-shaped. "I wonder if the ground is listening. If it has anything to say? God named the roots that he should feed the Indians. The water speaks the same way. God says feed the Indians upon the Earth. The grass says the same thing. Feed the Indians' horses and cattle. We do not order whites around, and they should not order us around."

Owhi of the Yakama stood. "God gave us day and night, the night to rest in, the day to see. As long as the earth lasts, he gave us the morning with our breath. He takes care of us on Earth. Shall I steal his land and sell it? Shall I give the lands that are part of my body and leave myself poor and destitute?"

Kamiakin lumbered up slowly, rising like a bear who knew no danger. "Now we know perfectly the heart of the Americans. It has not changed. They have hanged Indians for years without knowing whether we were right or wrong. When the governor speaks, I think of nothing but the weather. Many Yakama are not here. They are away. I do not tell them where to sleep."

The Indians crowded around their chiefs, dispersing, and Looking Glass cantered away, the Blackfoot scalp bouncing on its pole beside him, Lawyer following sullenly on foot.

Dominique and I ate supper beneath the governor's private arbor, letting the Nez Perce vote among themselves, and the governor opened McKalb's little metal box and went through the forms inside, McKalb watching discernibly.

"Five Crows," said the governor. "Young Chief. Stickus. Camaspello. Umhowlish. Who really rules the Cayuse?"

"It depends upon where they steal their horses and what kind of whoring they approve," said Agent McKalb.

"Whoring?" I said.

"There's three main bands," said McKalb.

"The Yakama think it's us who do the whoring," I said.

"What Yakama?" McKalb fingered a suspender testily. "Who? You got someone special telling you things? A squaw?"

The governor and Dominique stared my way, waiting, and I saw how clumsy I had been. "Yes, the Cayuse have three main bands," I said. "One up the Umatilla, another—"

McKalb guffawed, and the governor clanged the box closed, shutting it tightly. "No matter the chiefs or squaws, the Cayuse will go with the Wallawalla and the Umatilla," said the governor. "Away from Kamiakin and his hostiles." He quickly drew a map, sketching the third reservation-site, moving Kamiakin's boundaries north, adding a fishery on the Columbia. "The third reservation-site will prevent hot-headed Cayuse from cavorting with hostile Yakama every salmon season."

"The fish there belong to the Sinkiuse tribe, Chief Quiltenenock," said Dominique. "They speak Salish, not Sahaptin. They'll treaty with the Spokane."

"A Sinkiuse chief is nothing," said the governor.

"His band is nothing," said McKalb.

"The Sinkiuse belong to Kamiakin, and you forget, Dominique, this is America now," said the governor. "The Indians are conquered. They are no longer savages hunting beasts for Old World traders. Now they will farm in the New World."

Dominique rose heavily from his camp stool, his jowls drooping, his breasts suddenly looking aged, sagging against a sweat-stained blouse. The governor called for horses. We armed ourselves. We rode to the Yakama camp, where squaws worked busily, sewing bags for pack animals, carving stirrups, preparing to leave—Lalooh was sitting upon a blanket, stuffing horsehair into the pad of an Indian saddle, and she looked at me, then at McKalb, and her hands fumbled. She got mean-faced. She looked down, and suddenly braves grabbed our bridles, turning our horses, and Dominique shoved a shotgun against a brave's throat, and the warrior raised a hawk-nose, smiling snidely, the size of his grin nearly hiding his reach for his pistol.

Dominique shoved his shotgun deeper against him, and Hawk Nose tightened his grip on the bridle. Dominique rode on, staring only at Kamiakin's lodge, and the brave jerked and dropped the reins, Lalooh eyeing—almost ogling—him.

We rode on silently to Kamiakin's lodge and found the chief smoking inside, consulting with Chiefs Skloom and Owhi, and we sat upon robes opposite them, and Dominique spoke gravely, icily, launching into the treaty, pouring dire looks at the chiefs. "The aforesaid confederated tribes and bands of Indians hereby cede, relinquish, and convey to the United States all their right, title and interest... It is distinctly understood and agreed Kamiakin is the duly elected and authorized head chief of the Yakama nation."

"Many chiefs must agree," said Kamiakin.

"Even so, all the bands will stay strong from Kamiakin's wisdom," said McKalb. "Kamiakin already has gardens and ranches. He has already lived with Father Sidalia. He is the one to save all the Indians."

Kamiakin's eyes widened. "How does Young Andrew say it?"

The governor spoke curtly, and I translated, "The army sends five thousand troops presently. It will send troops until your people are no more. Can you stop the whites from coming? Can you stop the rivers from running?

The wind from blowing? Cannons will come here—and here—and here—and here. And if Kamiakin does not sign, every tribe will be destroyed, will look like the river-villages after small pox and fever. The Yakama will walk knee-deep in blood, and death will come like flies on a corpse."

Kamiakin sat searching our faces, and then he stared up through the lodge-hole at the dusky sky, swallows flitting, nighthawks ripping the air, booming like banners flapping. "The Indians shall stay on all their lands until the President says yes to the treaty and the reservations."

"Yes," I translated.

"No Indian shall be forced upon a reservation until the President says yes to the treaty."

"No, they shall not."

"No whites shall come between the Rockies and Cascades until the President says yes. They shall not build houses or fences."

"Yes, we will do everything we have said. No new land will be opened for settlement for two or three years. We have nothing more to say."

Kamiakin dipped a stick into ink, shaking visibly, biting his lip, and he marked the treaty, blood streaming down his chin.

Skloom and Owhi added marks, and we left and nursed mounts all through the night, visiting and haranguing chiefs, getting their consents until our mess fire licked the paling dark, and Lawyer strutted through our breakfast smoke, ostrich plumes flying triumphantly atop his stovepipe hat, Looking Glass walking in deference beside him.

"We now have the hearts of the Nez Perce," said the governor.

"And the stall of Kamiakin," said McKalb.

"Yes, you are correct, Thomas. Kamiakin will give horses to every warrior who joins him"

"He will use the delay in the treaty to gather guns."

"He foolishly thinks soldiers will not bother him during winter."

I went as if to the latrine pits. I crept through the willow, and Lalooh sat on her log as if waiting, staring over her shoulder, and I settled beside her, and she pulled a ball of dogbane twine from a beaded hemp bag, and she unraveled some twine, looping it with her elaborate primitive care upon her lap, grasping and feeling knots, counting to seven in Yakama. She came to a gap between knots—a week finished. She fingered a Russian bead—the day the ash had fallen from the sky, and her grandfather had said a new race of thieves would come from the rising sun. She unraveled loop after loop, yard upon yard. She fingered a red bead, her grandfather's death—then a dentalium bead, her mother's wedding—then two yellow beads, her grandmother's and sister's deaths—a shred of black cloth, first black gown at Yakama—a canvas-shred, the first wagons—a blue thread, the first soldiers.

The time ball had barely shrunk, and I wondered how far it went back, if it had started even before Columbus, and then Lalooh fingered the last knot, yesterday, and she raised her stare to mine, pooling her eyes deeply, beautifully, and I drew close, and then my head stung, and she held two of my hairs plucked between her fingers.

She tied them to the dogbane and left a crooked fork. "This is your mark forever." She stood packing the ball instantly. "The night you used our words against us." She hustled off, wagging her rump high like an antelope, swinging her head around, crying, and she vanished into willows thrashing from her haste, the green tips of branches lighting gold with the day's first rays.

2

Dominique, McKalb and the governor went north to take titles from the Spokane, Flathead, Pend d'Oreille and Blackfoot, but I did not speak their languages, and I took a flatboat down the Columbia, portaged lava beds to The Dalles, rode the Barlow Road to Six-mile Creek and followed sawmill noise into the towering-cool timber where Jake and his Indian boy were making boat-logs on his claim, planning to sell them to emigrants who would arrive this fall.

"Only fools will come this way this year," I said, and Jake showed me last week's *Pioneer and Democrat:* **Indians Cede Interior! Land Open to Whites!** I opened the newspaper to a territorial notice signed by the governor:

Donation Claims Available Outside New Reservation Boundaries

The country embraced in the cessions and not included in the reservations is open to settlement, except the Indians are secured in the possession of their buildings and implements until removed to reservations. Said tribes are to settle on their reservations within a year after ratification of the treaty; until then, Indians are allowed to occupy the tracts they now possess, and they will guarantee to all citizens of the United States the right to enter and occupy as settlers any lands not actually enclosed by said Indians.

I looked at the governor's map printed in the paper, and I counted days, and I figured he had dispatched the express from Mill Creek to Olympia even before the Nez Perce had voted. I realized the Walla Walla treaty could not have reached Congress or been ratified yet, and the thoughts wore me so thin

I stayed out of The Dalles and the hell-fire heat of the black-rock gorge all summer, and then the creek darkened with blue-backs, the willow yellowed, and I cut branches, making what Lalooh had called Coyote's traps, one-way fish baskets, and I hummed melancholy songs to myself, dreaming something gone, I guessed.

Though Father Sidalia had told me many times: "You cannot desire her forever. You cannot live like this, and she cannot." He and I had waded into Ahtanum Creek, reaching into rapids together, and we had pulled out a basket of blue-blacks, the fish slapping the willow-weave fiercely against our knees. "You must pray before you fish," he had said. "You must wake each morning and guard against her. You must lay in the dark, place your hand upon your chest— and grieve!" He caught his breath, stumbling on rock. "Smell not these salmon, Young Andrew! Smell the sulfur, the crackling smoke, the putrid things!" He gained the bank, stepping and lifting with me. "Hear the wailing, the howling, the blasphemies! Taste the tears of the dammed, all the bitter things! Feel the fire upon your flesh, the flesh of all sinners!" He quickened his voice, carrying the basket toward drying racks. "Carry not these salmon! But see yourself at Galilee! You have cast your net all night! It has risen empty! You have doubted! Yet now you feel the weight of what Christ has provided! You kneel before him!"

Sidalia and I dumped the blue-blacks upon tule mats, and Lalooh and her mother slit bellies with Hudson Bay's knives, kneeling, singing in choppy Yakama cries.

"Coyote wanted those women,
Oh, he wanted those five sisters,
Yes, they said, oh yes.

They became his wives,
They liked what he did.

Coyote put five rocks here,
He stopped the salmon here."

Sidalia bent above Lalooh, cupping his hands into a ball, his cassock clinging to his legs, dripping. "God reveals his wisdom to those who believe, Lalooh. Not coyotes, not wolves, not beasts. See? The world is round! White men sailed here on ships, put their faith in Him, let Mary shelter their passage! And so they saw how God made it so!"

His hands played tenderly with the shape of a ball. His dimples swelled their largest. He smiled, and a single finger stroked the air, shaking joyfully, and Lalooh and her mother looked up at me for help.

"He says the earth is not flat," I had said, and Lalooh's mother had shrieked. She had stood terrified. She had pulled her mat abruptly up-creek, calling for Lalooh to bring the fish and racks, and Sidalia had sighed in consolation, wringing the hem of his gown.

"Vanity of vanities, Andrew. All is vanity except loving God and serving God."

"Andrew!" Someone called my name. "Young Eaton!" I stopped humming. "Andrew Eaton! Jacob Eaton!" I lifted the fish basket, turning, and Father Sidalia sat high in sun-shafts beneath pines, stretching in his saddle, motes of hoof-dust settling and twinkling all around him, his robed figure clear in sunlight one moment, dark in the wind-shadows from boughs the next.

Jake walked to him—he was undeniably he, neither daydream nor apparition. He handed Jake a government note for logs. "Our Indians have broken out!" he said. "I had to ride in and tell Major Wells myself! I could send no one else!" Sidalia eyed the fish basket knocking my thighs, pouring icy water down my legs, and he frowned, hurrying me to drop it. He handed me down an express from the U.S. Army.

> "My honorable Andrew Eaton,
> The Department of the Pacific requests your immediate presence. Several parties of miners have been attacked by hostile Indians in Yakama country on the way to the Okanogan goldfields. At least six miners were killed at Naches Pass, early September, most likely by order of Kamiakin.
> Agent McKalb left the Spokane to investigate September 10 and has disappeared. Major Granville Haller and 102 troops and officers were dispatched to inquire the facts of the murders and the agent's disappearance, October 3. Haller has also failed to return, and I have

in my possession McKalb's saddle, brought in by a stable master who bought it from a Yakama squaw who claimed Haller and his entire force have been massacred.

Governor Curry has called for one thousand volunteers from Oregon. The governor of Washington has done the same, sending an express from the Blackfoot Council, Judith River, Montana Territory.

I guarantee the same rate for a civilian interpreter as Washington Territory (in gold).

I am sir,

Major E.G. Wells, commanding officer, Fort Dalles.

Eighth Infantry, Department of the Pacific."

Father Sidalia waited only until he saw my decision on my face, and then he galloped back downhill, heading to warn settlers on Seven and Eight Mile Creeks.

Three days later Jake and I moved logs by chutes and ox teams down to the fort, and while the quartermaster looked over the load, Major Haller marched his regulars up from the landing, his Dragoons leading sluggish mounts, corpses in blankets strapped to horse-rumps and wounded men in litters with dressings dust-laden and blood-sopped.

The foot soldiers followed gaunt-eyed, faces powder-burnt, scratched and gouged by burs and thorns, everyone with cartridge belts empty, no one smiling or speaking of the chief or agent they had failed to find, the cannon they had abandoned, or the fifteen hundred warriors who had run them out of Yakama territory.

Jake held our teams as the columns passed. "I will write Ma from here," he said. "When you come back, you can bring Lalooh up to the mountain, but no one else. I do not want any squaw or any more Indian family."

He took our oxen home, and I stabled my gray and bay and fought fleas in the hotel two nights, and then Major Wells received me in a mud-floor office so dark he burned lanterns at midday, his small-dark eyes as commanding a pistol-barrels, his bushy-blond brows apt to scowl, his spine as straight as his chair-back. "Kamiakin attacked Major Haller before he reached the mouth of the Ahtanum, fifteen miles south at Toppenish Creek," said Wells. "We will pursue him until we punish the Yakama, and we will also contact Father Sidalia at his mission. We suppose Kamiakin ordered the murder of McKalb. General Wool has commissioned three hundred fifty regulars, and the governor, three hundred fifty volunteers from Washington Territory and Oregon Territory."

"Agent McKalb took a very young squaw," I said.

I told Wells what Jake and I had seen.

"You did not actually witness the act, the two of them together?" he said.

"No sir."

Wells added notes to his report, writing without expression. "You will sometimes act as a guide and secretary as well," he said.

"Yes sir."

I signed the formalities, a private contract, and I embarked with the command early November, steam-boating across the Columbia, and we pushed up through the *Wahksum* Mountains, advancing along the route of Haller's retreat. We rode through the fall's first downpours, and on the sixth day we gained a summit of wet-blowing camas, and a Klickitat scout hollered from a leaning stand of larch, brilliantly gold, the mark of a spring unknown to whites. He signed to Wells and me, and we followed him down into a ravine to a fresh pile of brush, and he tossed off branches, jabbering, running his words, but I had no need to translate. The Indians had cut off McKalb's right hand and had stuffed it into his mouth, had poured his ink down his throat and had stuffed the jar and papers in too, and he lay dead in his underclothing, some parts rearranged and his manhood entirely absent.

"I've seen them do much worse, especially a devil like Kamiakin." The militia's leader—Major Benjamin Franklin Nicholson—clambered down into the ravine beside us, his blazing-red hair hanging drenched down his back, his beard dripping heavily, tangled and bushy halfway down his chest.

"You see Kamiakin's mark on this?" asked Wells.

"We're on his old ground," said Nicholson.

"Just like Chief George." Sergeant-colonel Phelps—a volunteer built as powerfully as a low-standing bull—joined Nicholson and glared down as the rain pounded McKalb's wounds white and pink and clean. "Chief George used this kind of savagery to shut down our mine on the Rogue—while it was giving up a half a bushel of gold a day. The Indians are banding against us everywhere."

"Down in the Siskiyous," said Nicholson. "Down the Columbia, down the coast, up around Puget Sound. One morning we'll wake, and they'll be inside our every cabin, aiming to kill all of us the same day."

"Kill us all and cut us all," said Phelps.

Wells winced and stiffened. "You are a sergeant-colonel?"

"Yes, he is," said Nicholson. "By power of the governor."

"The army has no such rank," said Wells.

"I gave it to him," said Nicholson. "He met the governor's call. He fought with me in south Oregon."

"Get up from that body, sergeant," said Wells. He turned to me. "Doctor Hammond will come down, and Company D will bury the body beneath boulders to be retrieved by a future detail."

"Company D of the Washington Militia?" said Nicholson.

"No, Eighth Infantry! Department of the Pacific! United States Army!"

The dark-brooding clouds ceased the next day, replaced by sunshine and dawn-frost, and we crossed Toppenish Creek uncontested and marched up the west bank of the Yakama River, and then braves galloped down a butte on the east bank, wearing only war paint, breech clouts and war bonnets. And squaws drummed on the ridge above them, yipping war songs in shrill-discordant screams, dancing between rocks, and I raised my spyglass and recognized no one, and I scanned the mouth of Ahtanum Creek and then the hills west, and I saw only sage and crumbling rock, but muskets popped behind me—braves were firing from the base of the squaws' ridge, their balls falling harmlessly in the bank-willow and river.

Wells halted the advance guard and sent word to the rear, and an old brave shouted in Yakama up on Squaw Ridge, dancing into open view, waving his arms in antics. Almcotty. *"The soldiers have come to be killed! They look like many on the plain, but they are bunched like a few rabbits surrounded by hunters and clubs! Hold your fire! Hold your ground! Kamiakin is coming! All his warriors! Thousands! We will wait until we can slay every soldier!"*

Little squadrons of braves charged downhill as if suffering buck fever. They fired muskets, shouted, gestured obscenely, returned uphill, and Sergeant-colonel Phelps and Lieutenant-major Taylor led Company D of the militia toward the river. They prepared to cross and charge, and Wells' buglers trumpeted, and regulars pulled cannon-guns from the backs of mules, slung them onto carts, pulled red-painted case shot from chests, took measurements with quadrants.

Our ammunition wagons, the pack train, beeves and spare stock entered an enclosure of tightly drawn pickets, and Wells, a couple colonels, Nicholson and I assessed our position from the center.

"Order Taylor to hold his position," said Wells.

"And let every squaw in the tribe escape?" said Nicholson. "There are not thousands of warriors up there, not enough rocks and bushes to hide them. I think they would have attacked us miles ago."

"You cannot charge that hill unless you get cannons across. You cannot possibly hold it without them."

"I beg you the honor, sir."

A second company of volunteers massed along the river, and Phelps turned at water's edge, pointing his saber above us, seeing what we could not, and I rode his way, reared, scanned west again, saw now breastworks built of stone as pale as the landscape, flanking our western line on both sides.

Kamiakin rose in his war bonnet from a bulwark about five hundred yards behind and above us. He waved two black flags, and Almcotty waved two more from Squaw Ridge. Wells' buglers played *squads right, squads left, squads into line.*

The blue-coats precisely formed, and Kamiakin stood with flags poised, seemed to stare in wonder at the music, the brass instruments, the gleam of the brass cannons, the gunners holding lanyards. Two more war bonnets rose from breastworks: Owhi, Skloom. The Yakama had never fought so many regulars, and none with medicine guns, you see. They had witnessed howitzers firing salutes at fur posts, but that was all. My heart throbbed. I scanned Squaw Ridge again, and it seemed as if Nicholson was right. Lines of braves rode down, but no squaw was anywhere now. They were probably fleeing with their families, Wells was giving them time, and I was hoping it was so, my courage weakening.

Kamiakin yelled down in trade language, *"Wake siáh mamaloose!" Death is not far away!*

Muskets popped from breastworks, and arrows arched high, whizzed down, and waves of braves came, shrieking, ducking and shooting from

34

behind mounts, and more shots popped from behind us, braves coming from the bottoms below Squaw Ridge, and *Boom! Boom! Boom!* Cannons lunged, smoking, deafening the air. Balls whistled east and west, shells burst above war bonnets, and Indians and their horses reeled, sprayed by clouds of shot, their bronze bodies splashing blood, sailing backward.

The Indians turned tail. They galloped east across Squaw Ridge. They scattered west toward the oaks above the breastworks, and a shell burst, lighting the air, and a mare threw a warrior, and he scrambled lizard-like, and Nicholson whooped, spurring his mount, leading a company, and they fell upon the brave, and Wells ordered me there, and I arrived as the men spread Old Weshanaberts on the desert floor, and Nicholson pressed an Indian scalping knife against his forehead, and Phelps grabbed and clawed a thigh.

Weshanaberts gazed up with cloudy eyes, though I had once seen them sparkle in a winter lodge, telling tales with Lalooh.

"Young Andrew," he said.

"Where is Father Sidalia?" I asked.

"Ran north."

"The other priests?"

"North."

"Are they prisoners?"

"Protected by their cross."

"Where are the rest of the warriors?"

Weshanaberts sang his death song.

"Kamiakin has too few warriors here. Where are the rest?"

Weshanaberts sang on.

"Where?" I said again, and Phelps inched a blade through buckskin of Weshanaberts' crotch, and others slowly stabbed his thighs, and then Weshanaberts' head sprayed blood, and Nicholson leaped up, waving a strip of flesh, the drops pelting my cheek, and I fingered my six-shooter, held it in my holster, saw one bullet in Nicholson's skull, another in Phelps' broad-muscled back, and then Nicholson shouted my name, ordered me downhill as if he commanded me, and I let go the trigger, grabbed reins and hurried to Wells and blue-coats racing down along Ahtanum Creek, shooting at squaws fleeing through brush, making for the river.

The blue-coats charged to the Yakama. Indians were jumping in above and below the creek's mouth. Lalooh was two-thirds across the current, stroking through rapids, sinking in a robe of fur, and a blue-coat knelt below me, shouldering his rifle, and I shouted, "The brave!" *Bang!*

A brave flew from a mount and floated limply—another old fellow, his gray hair splayed out. He snagged sideways a moment. He rolled face-up. Almcotty. He rolled down-current as Lalooh scrambled up a bank, and I emptied my chambers, aiming above her. She shook at the shots, scurrying into willow. She propped herself on all fours, dripping, gasping, and her eyes took me in, narrowing through the brush, hating, and she scrambled deeper into the brush, and then Yakama heads rose above bushes, riding, getting away, and shots rang all around me, and Wells shouted in my ear.

"Find Sidalia, Eaton! He'll know how many warriors there are, and where they are going! If the Yakama have him, tell them Major Wells will pay for him! Tell them they'll be moved safely to Fort Dalles!"

"Sidalia fled north, Weshanaberts said."

"Go see!"

I galloped toward the priest's cabin and reached it as smoke plumed through the roof, and flame-tips raced along shingle-edges.

Phelps and Taylor rushed out the door, Phelps wearing Sidalia's chasuble, Taylor his alb. They rode around the cabin. Phelps thrust up a cross, mocking it, and Taylor waved a bound-leather journal, Sidalia's Yakama dictionary. He pitched it onto the burning roof, whinnying in triumph.

Flames licked up the cabin's walls. They cracked and roared from the chapel, stable, the layman's cabin where Jake and I had lived, the Yakama lodges beyond. I dismounted, letting my gray shy from the fire, and I thought maybe Sidalia had been found inside, or some Indians were tied inside, and I turned to yell to Taylor or Phelps, but they were down in the garden now, Wells and Nicholson with them.

The heat was too fierce. I mounted again and rode down past a throng of volunteers throwing bags of flour onto a wagon—they had loaded on cases on wine, pulled out bottles, popped open corks.

I reached the garden as Wells, Nicholson, Taylor and Phelps watched a muddy-faced volunteer stoop in the cabbage patch and wrest a powder barrel out of the earth. Two men helped Muddy Face lift the barrel, one in a muddy clerk's vest and another in a muddy flannel shirt, muddy trousers. Muddy Face glared beseechingly at Wells, "Forgive me, sir, here's your proof. The priests have been arming the hostiles."

"Let go the barrel, all of you," ordered Wells. "You have no idea if the priests buried it to hide it from Kamiakin."

"Yes, we do, sir," said Muddy Face. "If the priests were against the Indians, the devils would have hacked them up like they did Reverend Whitman and his wife."

"Leave it, or I'll place you under arrest!" boomed Nicholson. "I broke bread with the reverend! I knew the half-breed who pulled Narcissa out of the ditch after she had been shot and whipped to death! The Whitmans lived peaceably until the bishop and priests came! It was they who incited the Cayuse against them!"

"Yes, look here!" Taylor thrust an open ledger into Well's hands. "Sidalia's accounts!" he cried. "He sold every Yakama brave a pound of powder every year!"

"You read French?" said Wells.

"In passing, sir."

"It says *shot* of powder, not *pound*."

"Well, Sidalia rides all over the country, and they don't touch him, do they?" said Nicholson.

Hogs squealed, and Muddy Face and Muddy Shirt wheeled and ran after them, aiming to catch our first fresh pork since Fort Dalles, and then more rifles clapped, horses and cattle screamed beyond the stable.

Wells barked at Nicholson, "Order your men to snuff their torches and stop shooting the Yakama stock, or they will be mustered out immediately, or hanged for treason!"

"Had you mustered us in soon enough, Agent McKalb would still be alive, and so would others!" said Nicholson.

Three Dragoons galloped whooping across the garden, looked at Wells and stopped, the color draining from their faces. The blue-coats stiffened in their saddles, one holding a smoking corn stalk, another a willow backrest from a lodge, the other an eagle-plume blanket. Wells flushed. "Relinquish those things to Quartermaster Haines, or you will pay for them with your commissions or your lives."

Wells ordered the horses rested a day, and we built rafts, crossed the Yakama with cable ropes the next morning and followed Kamiakin's tracks east across sage plateaus, moving against sleet, skirting old-dead Indians glazed in ice on frozen bunchgrass, a frozen papoose beneath antelope-brush, an old squaw sitting on the dry side of a gnarled juniper tree, singing, waiting to die, and I thought only of Lalooh and how to get her a message.

We crossed the Columbia thirty miles above its great bend to the sea, and we feasted upon Yakama horses butchered all along the bank—they had been left behind—some had drowned—others had frozen to death—others had been knocked to their ruin by the current—the wolves had already eaten their fill.

I woke the next morning feeling like a carload of dirt had been dumped upon me. My blanket and tent were too heavy to lift—snow had fallen and buried the Yakama's trail a couple feet under.

Wells turned us south, and we encamped at homesteads abandoned by whites, the fields and pastures smoky, reeking of black-smoldering snow, of tons of hay burned to keep the feed away from the Indians. More snow fell, and the Dragoons and the mounted militia broke the road, and the foot soldiers followed until the adobe walls of Fort Walla Walla loomed charred and misshapen against a low-leaden sky.

The stable and hay of the old post were in ashes, its stock loitered loose, the commissary stored nothing but the seed piles of mice. The factor's old quarters still stood but were furnished only with a letter rolled in oilskin, scrawled in haste: *I escorted the McKay, Gallagher, Blair, O'Ryan, Rutherford and Stedman families to Fort Dalles, November 15, 1855. Emmanuel Blair thought at least two thousand Yakama warriors were approaching. All the ranchers feared the Yakama would join with Peopeomoxmox and hostile Cayuse and Palus. They believed the Indians have already killed the governor, and the Spokane and other tribes will join the confederation and attack all whites. Yours dutifully, a servant of Washington Territory, Narcisse Purcell.*

Wells and Nicholson sent parties back up the Columbia to dissemble the homesteads' houses and barns, and the troops returned two days later with boards and logs and stood them endwise in trenches, commencing a new stockade.

Early one evening they hallooed and fired a cannon salute—Narcisse Purcell rode up the bank on a fleet and lovely charcoal mare, accompanied by a Nez Perce guard on an Appaloosa, and they pulled up below, anguishing, sizing up the fort's condition. Narcisse shouted, beckoning, and Wells, Nicholson and I hurried down, and we stared in shame at the cartons we had failed to notice beneath the emerald torrent congealing, knocking loudly with ice-chunks.

Narcisse spat petulantly—he was the same age as I, his jowls plump and bristly, his blue eyes derisive with scorn as he held his hands deep in the pockets of a fine cloth overcoat. "Four hundred pounds of powder," he said. "One thousand pounds of ball."

"Peopeomoxmox must have been drunk," said Nicholson.

"Wallawallas burned the fort, I'd say," said Narcisse. "But they did not toss in the ammunition. The Indian Department—McKalb—sent an express before I left. He ordered all ammunition thrown in, so no Indians or militiamen would steal it. The government thinks only regulars can shoot, but after the first settlers left, I stayed a month with half-breeds and kept the wolves at bay with my breechloader. Peopeomoxmox's braves trailed me, but they never dared approach."

Narcisse was a mixed-breed himself, of course, but white-skinned like his father, and he handed Wells an express in a gentlemanly manner, smiling cordially like Dominique, and we went up into Wells' office, the major gleaming his little-dark eyes inwardly, remaining silent until we settled ourselves on new chairs, wolf-hide seats.

"General Wool has suspended all military operations east of the Cascades until spring," said Wells.

"The general does not dictate policy here," said Nicholson. "The governor will write the President, and Wool will resign."

"No one has heard from the governor since he issued his call from the Blackfoot Council," said Wells. "He might have gone to New York or New Orleans to catch a steamer back, rather than brave the winter snows of the Rockies."

"The governor does not fear the snow on any mountain in the world," said Nicholson.

"My father will bring him across," said Narcisse.

"We will wait for them here," said Nicholson. "And hunt the hostiles."

"Congress will not pay your militia another cent," said Wells.

"Congress will call us heroes," said Nicholson.

"I cannot enforce treaties which are not yet known to be ratified," said Wells. "My companies depart tomorrow."

"And mine remain," said Nicholson, and he looked at me gamely, towering his brow and eyes, and I realized I might deliver my message in person: *The willows have already turned bare, my sweet Lalooh, and they will not hide you forever. I aimed high, Lalooh, so you could escape to be my wife, a free Indian woman on a white man's claim. I have saved passage on a ship to the east, Lalooh, so we can live on settled land in peace until the war between our people ceases.*

And so the first week of December I rode south up Mill Creek with Major Nicholson while Lieutenant-major Taylor searched east up the Walla Walla and north up the Touchet.

And I gathered with troops beside the sink of the old mill pond as Nicholson climbed upon a wagon-bed and took off his beaver hat and held it solemn against his blue-wool overcoat, a cold-cutting wind turning his face the color of his beard, chasing clouds one moment and blowing flurries the next, whistling between the bare-wooden rails, sweeping the grave markers. "The first white baby in all of Oregon and Washington Territories—Alice Clarissa Whitman—was born right here," he said. "When she was almost three, she came to her mother before a Sunday supper. She begged her mother—Narcissa Whitman—the first American woman to cross the Rockies—to fetch water for the supper. She went right over there to the river." Nicholson let his gaze wander and rest dolefully on the spot on the bank. "And when she did not return, the reverend and his wife did not dwell for long on their despair. They recognized Providence, and Narcissa said, '*The Lord has taken our own dear child away, so we may care for the poor outcasts of the country.*'"

"She and Reverend Whitman took in Joe Meek's daughter and Jim Bridger's too. They took in the seven children of a mother crushed beneath a wagon and a father killed in two hours by the shitting disease. They took *me* in, and though they sent me to the Lapwai Mission before the Indians killed them, I remember the prayer Narcissa spoke whenever a Cayuse tramped into her kitchen and left his dirt upon her linen. `Lord, let not this mission fail.`

"And now General Wool and Major Wells have left us to find and fight the Indians alone, and I tell you the same. `Lord, let not this mission fail.`" Nicholson pulled the beaver hat from his chest and dug out a string of scalps, held and shook it high, pointed at each. "Rogue from Jacksonville. Piute from the Pitt. Shoshone from the Snake. Yakama from the Yakama." He held up a second string. "All Cayuse!" The troops let go a mighty cheer, and Nicholson opened his palm for quiet, smiling, forgiving our mistake, letting the scalp-strings dangle from a finger.

We were to make no extra noise, you see. Nicholson had forbidden our hunters to fire guns, and so we were fed a soup of vegetable bricks as dry and musty as hay, of knotty-stringy beef, and we snuffed our fires and slept six to a tent, shivering against frozen ground, rolling upon one another all night, and I woke at four, boiled coffee, skimmed the weevils from it, and Sergeant-colonel Phelps led my gray out of the sink through the dark, beckoning silently, urgently. He had ridden from Taylor's battalion, leaving at midnight. He put my reins in my grip, and I was off with him before daybreak, accompanied by Nicholson, and we retraced our route of the previous day, the rest of our force to follow immediately.

We forded the Walla Walla, met Narcisse on the north bank, rode up the road to a hillock at the base of a butte, and we dismounted, and a bare human heart lay dripping red drops on a fresh dusting of snow, surrounded by six small circles drawn around it and then by a single encompassing loop.

"A sign of Indian federation." Narcisse pointed at sticks lined up inside the small circles. "Those four sticks mean four hundred Yakama warriors. Those four, four hundred Cayuse warriors. Those three, three hundred Palus and Wallawalla warriors—two hundred Klickitat—one hundred Sinkiuse—all unified by Kamiakin."

We rode up a hill that commanded a view of the river and the road. We passed Indian breastworks and rifle pits, and Taylor hailed us from the top, and he brought us to lodge-scars and smoldering fires, and Narcisse seized a spade and dug down through fresh coals, a few feet of yellow dirt, layers of straw and grass. He squatted, knifed open boxes of tules, tore black-moss wrappings from *kouse* and camas.

"We found barrels of army-issue pork," said Taylor, "army-issue corn and army-issue flour. We found Hudson's Bay boxes—ink powder, foolscap, candles, files, pencils."

Phelps drove a shovel through another pile of coals. He dug deep and finally pulled out an Indian barrel made of cottonwood. He reached in and flung a pouch-cradle onto snow, baby moccasins stuffed with fur, a tiny comb made of willow sticks. He threw cooking sticks, digging sticks, a heron-bone flute onto the snow. He held up cooking baskets. "These ain't Wallwalla. They're Yakama or Cayuse. They had squaws here too."

"Peopeomoxmox watched us turn south yesterday," said Nicholson, "and then he saw the lieutenant-major coming, and he ran for Kamiakin."

Taylor led us across the hilltop to troops dismantling piles of stones—one man yelped, turning, nearly stumbling with a box he had opened—rattlesnake heads lay inside, the fangs glistening against frozen-yellow skin.

Another man pulled quivers from the same pile of stones. "Venom," he said. "Poison arrows."

Another man picked through war paints and war vests. "Forgotten sorrows," he said.

We found winter stores of elk and antelope and boiled the meat with camas, and the rest of our men arrived, and we ate root cakes and soup until we were full and warm. We allowed our mounts all the corn they wanted and then proceeded as a single unit up the Touchet, the temperature rising above freezing, the snow turning slushy, showing deep-sloppy tracks.

We followed the galloping retreat of Peopeomoxmox, his sentries watching us from ridges. We skirted a little-tumbling falls, and warriors on the heights got as thick as blackbirds, no squaws or kids anywhere—already out of the way.

We turned a little east of north, and the blackbirds swooped down—bucks with spears, rifles, muskets and headdresses, their bodies and horses colored for battle, no matter the paints left behind. We halted, and the Indians sang a high-crying war song, banging sticks, hooting and yipping—there were maybe sixty, we were nearly three hundred. They formed an arc of a line just out of rifle range, and five kept coming—Peopeomoxmox in the lead, waving a white handkerchief.

Narcisse, Taylor, Nicholson and I rode out and waited, and Peopeomoxmox reared before the major, wearing his derby, not his war cap. His sub-chiefs drew beside him, and he flared his nostrils at Narcisse, disdaining him with the same contempt he had shown Dominique at the council—he would no more trust his words to the trader's boy than he would to Master Purcell—he could not forget how Dominique had falsely promised that whites would find and punish the man who had shot his son on the Feather River.

Nicholson cocked his fiery beard toward the war party, I translated. "Why do you wave that white flag?"

"Peace," said Peopeomoxmox.

"You have burned a trading post and stolen stock and provisions," said Nicholson.

"The governor talked very bad to us," said Peopeomoxmox. "He said we must be penned on reservations, and I felt like a feather blown away. The governor made war on the Yakama, and then he sent the settlers away, so he could make more war on the Wallawalla."

"The governor did not send away the settlers," said Nicholson. "You burned them out. You sent your squaws and children away today."

"No, we will have peace today." Peopeomoxmox gestured behind his warriors toward a long rocky pass. "We will sleep in peace tonight. You will smoke with us up there tomorrow. We will have a talk."

"We have found our provisions in your pits," said Narcisse.

"If my braves stole things, they will be whipped," said Peopeomoxmox. "The things will be returned, or I will pay in gold and horses."

"You must put down that flag and surrender, or you must fight," said Nicholson. "You are stalling, hiding Kamiakin. We saw the heart upon the snow. We know you have joined the Yakama and Cayuse and other tribes against us. We saw your village, how you planned to mass warriors there and block the road."

"The road was built upon Wallawalla land," said Peopeomoxmox. "The treaty allows us to live north of the river."

"The road is also for whites and the Nez Perce," said Nicholson. "You must surrender and come with us and tell your people to council tomorrow at your old winter village. We will be waiting with our cannons up there. We will not fire them if you and your chiefs stay with us."

Hooves stirred behind us. Phelps led a string of privates on prancing mounts—the men flapped arms, sighted rifles at warriors, crowed as if to imitate war cries—the warriors whooped in return, pumping guns and bows, riding nearer.

"Major," said Peopeomoxmox, "I see your boys are like mine. They are keen for a fight. But I am old, and you are wise, and we have more sense." He drew his horse beside Echo, an old Wallawalla sub-chief, and he mumbled fast and low, handing him the white flag, and Echo rode back toward the warriors, holding the handkerchief high.

Phelps and his men circled around us, cocking hammers, taking aim, and Nicholson and Taylor moved from chief to chief, taking their rifles and pistols and knives, and Peopeomoxmox slitted his eyes, bearing the insults silently.

Nicholson barked at Phelps, "Keep them in the center of the line!" He barked at me. "Stay with them! If they talk battle-talk, stop them!"

Our line turned about, and Nicholson rode to the front, leaving Taylor to the rear, and we proceeded at a trot down the west bank of the Touchet, and warriors followed us on the east side, staying high on the slopes, riding just below the spindly-black columns of lava rock on top, never out of sight.

Peopeomoxmox held his head defiantly, his face and chest rising nearly as thickly and resolutely as Kamiakin's. His hair was strung with beads and feathers, his face rippled stubbornly with courage, his eyes roamed distantly. He might have seen all the way to Sutter's Fort, the story all of us knew. His son Toayahnu had been killed unarmed. Toayahnu, Peopeomoxmox, Spokane Garry and other Indians had dressed themselves like company men and had gone to hacienda country to buy white cattle. But they had won horses from hostile Indians instead, and Toayahnu had been shot while kneeling outside an adobe church, praying before a clerk of Sutter's who had seen a mule of his in the Indian's herd.

Suddenly our line broke into a gallop, and a few braves kept pace, riding along the bank across the river, shouting words too fast to catch. Peopeomoxmox and his sub-chiefs shrieked, their yips rattling wildly, hissing, clacking, and then Phelps was gone, only his men were with me, and shots popped from the front, the rear too, and we kept the prisoners between two lines, squeezing them from both sides.

And then the opposite bank opened into a flat, and Wallawalla were descending slopes to it, firing, and a wall of rock rose on our side, and Peopeomoxmox worked his reins, turning into me, and we swung sharply into the Touchet, and we joined a chaos of mounts, horses splashing, squealing, snorting, troops shouting and whipping quirts, and then we ascended the east bank, riding desperately, the chiefs still with us, the Wallawalla warriors still on our left, pulling ahead of us, inviting pursuit.

And then the hill of the village site passed behind us, and Cayuse warriors charged down it, Blue Hawk their war chief was at our rear!

We raced the Indians for miles, and Peopeomoxmox sang and chanted. He shouted through sudden flurries of snow, *"Sk'ulúput!" Whirlwind! "Páshtin!" White man! "Súltsas!" Soldiers! "Piitl'iyawit!" Killing!* He mixed in other words, yelling as if making commands, and I clung to reins, shunning my pistols, not risking a fall, not inclined to draw. I looked at the chief, and he invited my fear, my contempt, and I spurred my gray, and I then saw a blue-coated man standing up high ahead, big flakes of snow swirling around red-blowing hair, Nicholson's beard a bright-blowing target.

Nicholson stood in his stirrups, waving his beaver hat—no, he stood upon a rail, holding a post, hailing us toward a gate, rifles smoking and flashing around him, the barrels poking through a fence.

We had come to Mathieu's Ranch, the claim of a company man who had fled after the treaty. The chief raced past the major, I followed through the gate, and we veered from teamsters snapping whips, artillery wagons banging, hurrying to positions.

Phelps galloped beside me again. "The cabin!" We spurred toward chimney-smoke, and we came to troops waiting, shouldering rifles, and we halted, and the men pulled down the chiefs, shouted, pushed them, and I swung off, and Phelps offered a hand, hurrying me into the cabin—Taylor and Narcisse were inside, aiming rifles at the chiefs—the chiefs stood snarling from the rear wall, their brown skins sweating, the stove ticking with heat, Peopeomoxmox still looking defiant, leaning this way and that, trying to see out the door.

Nicholson and a private stepped across the threshold, the latter bleeding from a shoulder, his arm dangling. "I need every man at a post!" cried Nicholson.

"What about the prisoners?" said Narcisse.

"Keep them out of the way! Shoot them or tie them, I don't care which!"

Nicholson and the private turned into the snow again, hurried toward gunfire, and Phelps stepped up, flexing a rope, and Peopeomoxmox yelled in broken English. "No tie men! No tie chiefs! Tie dogs! Tie horses!"

"Hands up!" said Narcisse, and Peopeomoxmox reached down, and Narcisse swung his rifle. The steel of the barrel banged solidly. Bone cracked. The barrel clanged against the floor, and Narcisse raised a broken breech, and the chief lay on the puncheons, his sub-chiefs shouting, scuffling with Phelps as he and others shoved them, beating them with gun-butts, wrapping and tying them.

Peopeomoxmox raised himself slowly to his knees, his head drooping. An Indian knife lay by his feet—pulled from his legging? Narcisse stooped, rose, smashed the barrel against the chief's head again. The chief lay limp again, and guns blasted, and the other chiefs flew against the rear wall. They slumped and moaned amid powder smoke. They writhed and bled on the floor as the shots rang and lingered in my ears, and Narcisse hunched above Peopeomoxmox, the Indian knife firm in his grasp. He slashed the chief's scalp, cheeks, ears. He sliced open the chief's robe, and Phelps whooped, joining Narcisse, and then Taylor and others piled on, working blades, and pops and sucking sounds ripped loudly, flesh coming off bones and innards. Narcisse leaped up, waving a razor-strap of skin, his face and clothes smeared with blood, and he tossed brown-skinned privates on the stove—the chief's scrotum, testicles, penis. They hissed moistly there, frying, the black hair singeing, stinking, skin burning, smelling of blood, piss, sex, and I stood heavy-legged, two revolvers drawn, aimed at the mutilated chiefs, ready to fire the moment any one of them stirred and showed any capability.

"Eaton!" Taylor knelt up, screaming, waving one of Peopeomoxmox's braids, ordering me outside.

I roused myself. I went out with Taylor, and we moved through troops priming muskets and rifles, dragging cannons by ropes, loading shells, and we drew beside Nicholson, and Taylor handed him a strip of flesh on a bayonet. "The chief! Old Peopeomoxmox! Old Yellow Serpent!"

The cannons boomed tremendous blasts. They went off in perfect time together, the shells screaming from all sides of the ranch, flashing yellow and white in the blowing snow. We waited. Nothing stirred in the blowing snow, nothing on the ground, nothing in the air. Nicholson barked, waving the strip of flesh, and I yelled his words, the wind whistling, howling cold and bitter again, the flakes flying into our eyes.

"Your scoundrel chiefs have died for their deceptions! They have been gelded like useless-old bulls! We have cut them to pieces just as we will sever your entire nation into useless bits!"

We moved to every cannon station. Nicholson waved the bayonet, and I shouted, and the flurries ceased as abruptly as they had begun. The sky opened blue and bare, and snow blew in great racing clouds from the ground, blurring the sage and gulches and buttes, and we neither saw nor heard any of the enemy.

Nicholson boomed in the morning. "Company D! A! E! F! H!"

Half our mounted force gave chase through three more snowfalls.

We searched north to a rim above the Snake and encountered neither Peopeomoxmox's Wallawalla nor Kamiakin's Yakama nor Blue Hawk's Cayuse. We found only lodge-rings, stock-scars and then trails scattered down a sheer canyon wall into a howling abyss swept by bitter-cold gusts of pelting snow, and then we turned and made for the fort on gimping-starving horses, some blinded, others snorting icicles, their hocks bleeding from ice cuts, and we heard the Columbia before we saw the stockade, the river below thundering a constant-muffled growl, the ice on top wailing and twanging like a gigantic saw blade, banging so loudly and suddenly the horses shied, and I waited for the earth to split open, the sky to weep like a grieving squaw, the world to flood with wrath.

And one day a long line of snow clouds appeared on the plateau north of the fort, rising in cold so deep the clouds hardly billowed or sank beside the governor's pack train, and I thought there must be hope, *something*, as Dominique rode up and dismounted, smiling wryly through an ice-laden beard as Nicholson and another volunteer lifted the governor gingerly from his saddle, propped their arms beneath his old rupture, carried him inside.

Dominique threw arms around Narcisse, brimming his eyes with long-suspended joy, even rapture, and then he chuckled, embracing me like a second son, and he and I took up picks, and we broke the frozen earth, digging a pit, and we rode down to the bank and cut and wove willow.

"I saw Quiltenenock," said Dominique.

"The Sinkiuse chief?"

"Yes, he said governor has no right to give his land and fishing rights to Kamiakin, but the governor refused to see him. He forbade me from translating for him."

We went up to our pit, put our willow dome on top, heated rocks, and the governor came out and sat bare-legged in the sweathouse, untying his hernia truss, and he groaned in delicious relief, his over-sized forehead gleaming lobster-red, beading drops, his smile hugely white, glowing with the success of treaties signed in nearly all of the new northwest.

"When I met the Spokane, Chief Garry thought I wasn't real." The governor passed cups of warm-mellow brandy. "He thought Kamiakin had already killed me, and I was my ghost."

Narcisse and Nicholson tossed their heads, "Ha-ha-ha-ha-ha!"

"Chief Victor claimed the Flathead pray to a blue jay," said the governor. "They think the bird brings the spring wind up the Columbia and to the Rockies."

Narcisse and Nicholson laughed, "Ha-ha-ha-ha-ha!"

"The Blackfoot say their medicine pipe flew down from Pleiades and landed in a chief's lap," said the governor.

"Ha-ha-ha-ha-ha!"

Narcisse raised and swirled a jar of white alcohol, a brown nose, ears and thumbs floating inside. "To the defiance of Peopeomoxmox," he said, and Dominique abruptly stood, yanking up Narcisse, and the willow-dome flew off, the jar smashed in the pit, and Narcisse flew backward, sprawling down hard, and he pushed himself up slowly, setting his feet firmly, his chest bare and heaving, and Dominique paced bow-armed to him, clenching his fists deliberately, his feet crisply crunching snow. He struck like a disciplined boxer. He beat Narcisse's face, driving him backward, the blows slapping like wood, echoing, and the governor leaped, and Nicholson and I caught his arms, and he bucked like a salmon in a net, heaving powerfully.

Narcisse spat blood at Dominique, his nose and lips bleeding, one of his eyes closed, his cheeks dripping blood as well. He raised both fists, nodding eagerly, and he moved in, and Dominique feigned left, let loose a battery, and Narcisse spun and fell face-first, and the governor yelled, thrashing in our grips, "Stop, stop at once! He is your boy, your son!"

Dominique scowled over a shoulder, "My son's soul does not belong to

America. It does not belong to you. It belongs to civilization." He tugged his drawers straight to his waist and marched on high-arched feet down an ice-packed path toward the quarters as if he still factored the post.

Dominique continued to take meals amiably at the governor's table, and he pored over maps with him, deliberating how supplies from the blockhouse at the Cascades could be barged up the Columbia during spring, how five hundred regulars and five hundred volunteers might drive all the hostiles north to Canada. He took tea with Nicholson and the governor every day, and one morning two quick shots rang outside the stockade, then two slow, and he and the governor descended the wagon road cut in the snow. They hastened to Narcisse mounted in wolf-skins—he led a second horseman who tottered rigidly, a long wisp of a beard gleaming icily, his boots appearing frozen to stirrups, a dark gown frozen to the goat-skin on an Indian saddle.

I fired the sweathouse, and Dominique and Narcisse slid Father Sidalia through the door-flap and onto robes, and Dominique knelt above him, pressing his lips against his mouth, blowing in breath, and the governor laid a palm against the priest's neck, searching for his pulse.

"He was five miles out, dead-looking already." Narcisse spoke leaving. "His horse was coming in on her own."

Dominique grabbed the cassock and pulled it off by its hem, the wool spitting ice from stockings and underclothes, clinking and popping, and Nicholson ducked in, handing me whiskey, and I dashed it upon Sidalia'a chest, for we had no turpentine. We rubbed the whiskey into his skin, and he felt as cold as Pa the day Jake and I had found him, and I thought Sidalia as dead as Pa, but the whiskey warmed as we worked it, and Dominique bent mouth-to-mouth again.

Dominique sat up, and Sidalia parted his lips, gawked confusedly about and stared at Nicholson's beard. "You were at the mission."

"And you?" said the governor.

Sidalia's stare sharpened toward the voice. "Governor, you have returned? You are alive?"

"By the grace of God. We have not met in heaven yet, my friend."

"Quiltenenock—"

The governor raised a hand, nodding Sidalia down, shushing him, and Sidalia sank beneath robes, easing his head into Dominique's grasp, and he breathed evenly, seemed to recognize me as well as Dominique.

Dominique raised a whiskey cup to his lips, and Sidalia sipped, sank again, seemed to quiet toward sleep.

"I will wait by him, then Andrew, then myself again," said Dominique. "He knows us best. If Doctor Hammond had not left with Major Wells, we might do otherwise, but this man must be attended."

"He watched his mission burn." Nicholson slung off his coat, settled himself comfortably as if to remain. "He watched his Indians maneuver against us on the field. He armed and spied for them, I bet."

Sidalia sighed audibly, rousing at the rebuff. "Lo, you might have killed all of us, every priest and brother, but Kamiakin warned us, and we fled. We watched the fire from a hill, and we thanked God for our lives and then walked up the Columbia alone. Some Sinkiuse fed us the fourth day, and we reached St. Paul's at Kettle Falls the eighth."

"No one would have killed you at your mission," said the governor. "But rest, father, sleep. We will have ears tomorrow too."

"No, please, send a wagon north—blankets, flour, soda, meat, coffee," said Sidalia. "I left fifty friendly Indians at the Blair place, Sinkiuse and Yakama. They are afraid the war will push north of the Snake, and they want to winter with the Nez Perce."

"Fifty friendlies? By what authority, Father?"

"By authority of their hunger—and God's kindness."

"You are transporting Indians who in no way have proven they have not taken part in Kamiakin's war. I might arrest you."

"They are squaws, boys, girls, a handful of baptized warriors."

"Your Indians must come in and surrender. You can recover, Father, and then you must turn around. You must remain absent from Yakama country until Kamiakin has been conquered. You must remain north of the treaty line and of the Snake. Otherwise you will be arrested."

Sidalia sank beneath robes and raised a hand, and the governor took it. "Governor, behold a man stripped of his raiment, bleeding upon the road at Jericho!" Sidalia spoke in halting wisps of breath. "You bind his wounds! You pour oil and wine onto him! You mount him upon your own beast and bring him to an inn! The mercy of Christ swells in you, the miracle of Mary!"

"I have no wagon of goods," said the governor. "The army has left me none. I will send word to your Indians, and they will come here and answer questions about Kamiakin's federation. They will be prisoners, and I will feed them what I can, and then they will guide me to Kamiakin, or they will die." He bent to Sidalia's hand and lightly kissed it, Nicholson grimacing, loosening shirt-buttons, dripping sweat as the willow-dome heated up.

The governor leaned to Dominique. "Sidalia's Indians will listen best to the old trader and his son, I think. You and Narcisse will go to them, escorted by A Company." He looked at me. "You will watch over Father Sidalia, and I will post a guard. Send for me immediately if the father speaks again of the Yakama."

I fetched wood as they left, and a guard brought broth, and I sat by Sidalia, smelling the thin scent of beef and salt in the gruel, hungering with my own questions, and suddenly his eyes burned directly at mine, and he drained the broth readily and smiled wanly, his dimples shining scarlet, blistering, frost-bitten. "She is not at the Blair place," he said. "I hear nothing of Kamiakin's Yakama. No one tells me."

"She swam the river just as Almcotty was shot," I said.

"God punishes, Andrew. God gives. God takes. He does what He does. Even if you only have the grace of God, you must remember you have everything."

No Indians were found at the Blair place, only a trail north. Sidalia left for St. Paul's on a bitter morning ten days before Christmas, and had the weather warmed, the governor would have led us along the priest's route to hunt again for Kamiakin. But on New Year's Day he took the necessary measures to limber himself for a long stint in the saddle to Olympia, so I walked—raced—beside him, jotting blindly beneath the stars as he paced circles inside the stockade, the first white hue of the dawn-glow still three hours away, the teamsters packing the governor's train by torchlight.

He dictated a letter to Jefferson Davis, Secretary of War: "*General Wool in his comfort at Benicia is content to play the part of the dog in the manger, neither to act himself nor to let others act. He has refused us oats, and thus our horses freeze to death standing in snow too deep and iced over to rustle. He has refused* us provisions, and thus my troops suffer shoddy buildings, dejection, anemia and scurvy. Hundreds of warriors in violation of last spring's treaty remain poised to swoop in and murder me and prevent settlers from cultivating and planting this spring. Yet Wool keeps Wells' regulars at Fort Dalles, so they can catch syphilis from tavern-squaws."

As the sun rose, the governor mounted a horse beside Dominique, and both nodded admirably at each other, pulling wolf-skin muffs over noses, staring with mutual resolve at Nicholson and the troops seeing them off. The governor stood in stirrups, lifting a hand in farewell. "Though the army denies us howitzers—denies us shot and powder and hardtack and rifles—we will ship them upriver in spring!" He pulled his muff farther from his mouth, gesturing as if he were tipping a hat to the troops. "Until then—do not be summer soldiers like the regulars! Never—never abandon a line! Only bold and repeated charges will evict the savages! Only courage and duty! Only in this way can we achieve the superiority of our race!"

Narcisse appeared only as the train's last snow-clouds sank on the southern horizon, and he smelled of the inside of the gutted mare he had used as a blind, of the panicked innards of the wolf whose skin he carried—rangy and rutty.

"My father lives too many lies," he said. "He thinks he can still run a post the way the company taught him at York, but he stays so small he cannot see the size of the governor and his mission. He wants merely to survive, to keep the company's old monopoly on trade. He cannot see how greatly the governor changes the world, how he stands up to vile savages who sign treaties only to shoot from behind them, who have always practiced bigamy and stolen whiskey—no, he cannot see how greatly the governor opens the new western empire to Christ."

And I thought of Pa lying beside the frozen Sandy, snow brushed from his face, eyes popped open, tufts of blanket-wool stuck to his whiskers, the snow above him untrammeled—no bird or animal tracks—the drifts just peacefully curved as if he had merely lain down to rest, having no fear of dying after leaving our farm to hunt, snow-shoeing halfway up the Sandy toward Mount Hood.

"You believe in Christ?" I asked. "Life after death? The truth of the Lord?" Narcisse laughed. "You?"

The terrain below us sloped so frozen, and sage and greasewood stood so cold and skeletal-looking I could not seriously think of Pa's rising soul or Christ on a hot-desert cross. I could only shrug and feel secretly plucky, knowing I had forsaken a chance at going home, the warmth of Jake's cabin, and instead I had remained perhaps an honest fool, still staying, believing in a red angel and a pledge.

Nicholson wanted a new stable built to protect stock.

And so Narcisse and I went with Lieutenant-major Taylor and Company D up the Walla Walla and then Dry Creek, looking for suitable cottonwood, and when squaw-knives knocked echoing through a defile, I scouted ahead and lay alone on a ledge and spy-glassed two Yakama lodges deep down in a narrow bottoms, horses chewing on lower branches, a broad-cheeked squaw stripping bark, feeding it to a roan, a second squaw hacking branches, a third wearing a pregnancy belt, piling the sticks. The horses had no brands, were not ours, and I wondered if braves watched me secretly, and I tried to think of a lie to tell Taylor and Narcisse to get everyone safely across the river of blood I saw coming, and I recalled instead Dominique's canoes at the Umatilla, the need for a leak-proof truth, and then a hawk cried, lofting itself from a cottonwood-crown, and the pregnant squaw looked up, seeing perhaps my spy-glass hanging over the rim, and she raised her cheeks and braids, blowing cold-air vapor like Lalooh the night I had met her, and then she looked right—a brave stepped out of each lodge, the warriors wearing buffalo-skin hats with ear-flaps—one carried a willow switch for horse-rumps, the other a hatchet to break ice on the creek.

The pregnant squaw looked at the hatchet-brave, and they both looked up and past me, and a snow-clod dropped from the rim—Narcisse had flushed the hawk, trailing me—he stood now behind a pinnacle of rock, training his sight down, and he fired, and breechloaders clapped all along the rim. The hatchet-brave flew against his lodge, grabbing a hip, and then he collapsed, hit again, his face banging snow, his hat flying, and the other squirmed upon his back, losing his switch, his limbs waving uncontrollably, and a second fusillade followed, and then the braves and two squaws lay unmoving in scarlet pools, and the pregnant squaw crawled beneath her pile of branches, dragging a foot, blood leaking from a winter moccasin.

"Leave her!" ordered Narcisse, and the truth finally occurred to me.

"They're friendlies!" I bellowed. "Just wintering where there's horse-feed!"

"They're a-hundred miles east of the governor's line!" shouted Lieutenant-major Taylor.

"Violating his treaty!" said Narcisse.

The company went down to the defile, and Sergeant-colonel Phelps fired, his bullet pinging off rock, spraying chalk, and the echo rang around us, and the wind howled a hollow whine, knocking around the treetops, whistling against canyon-walls. Phelps had aimed at a shadow, and we saw no one up high, no one by the creek. We heard no death moans. The lodges came into view, and sticks banged. The pregnant squaw crabbed along on her stomach, and Narcisse sprinted to her. She lifted a pointed stick to her juggler, and he stepped on her arm, taking the stick.

"Eaton!" cried Taylor. "Tie off her foot!"

I cut a strip from a dead brave's legging and fixed it above her ankle, the squaw lying limp, her eyes unblinking, her breath subdued, Narcisse still stepping on one arm, Taylor the other. "Hoist her," said Taylor, and I lifted one leg, and Phelps the other, and Narcisse and Taylor took her arms, and we carried her into her lodge and laid her between furs. And Taylor put a revolver in my hand, nodding for me to sit beside her, and I did so, and he piled logs on the lodge-fire and stripped in sudden-blazing warmth, a lanky man with his manhood long and drooping, his skin as pale as a day-time moon, his ribs showing, and he got hard, grinning at the squaw, his teeth loose and crooked, his gums bloody and swollen with scurvy.

Narcisse waved her suicide stick back and forth. He drew a knife and pared the point sharper, and I aimed the gun at the squaw, and she gritted her nose, daring me, and I spoke Yakama as coolly as I could. *Did she know Kamiakin? His whereabouts? His plans? His federation?*

She peered silently down at her belly beneath the fur, and then Taylor crawled in, pawing her, nipping her chin, and she jerked away, and he spat and delivered a fist, cracking her shoulder, and he lowered himself and thrust his loins upon her, rocking, thrashing, and he grunted cow-like, rolling off, leaving a couple loose teeth where he had mouthed her hair.

I asked my Yakama questions again, and the squaw swung her head sideways, closing her eyes, and then Phelps stood, pushing his trousers down thighs still stout from working mountain claims, but ridden with rashes, sores seeping scurvy-blood, his manhood thick and ready, arching up hog-nosed. He stared at the squaw, waiting for her to look at him. "I had this once at the mines for a-half cup of sugar, and her brave got so mad he gouged out one of her eyes." Phelps swept broad-cupped fingers through chestnut hair, his stomach beating with panting breaths, and then he got in, thumbing her shoulders and face, nosing her roughly, and Donaldson from Ohio came next, Stewart from Kentucky, Brown from Cow Creek, and finally she lay as slack as a fish too-long on a bank, her nose and mouth all mush and blood, and I thought and acted out my lie. I shook my head as if disgusted by her silence, and I went out, leaving only Narcisse and his pointed stick in there, and she screamed, "*Xuun! Yayk!*"

We burned her body and the others and everything else of no use to us, and Narcisse and Taylor rode buoyantly on the way home, leading the company double-file, commiserating, and I lagged behind our wagon of lodge-poles, not wanting words with anyone, for I had not yet known the act of love with a woman, nor witnessed it before in a human way, and bile leapt in my throat, and I hung backward over my gray mare, retching, and when we sat before Nicholson at the fort, he eyed the vomit stains on my shirt.

"Seattle has been attacked," said Nicholson. "The governor sent word. Leschi and his band of Nisqually drove all the whites to one end of town and tried to board the *Decatur*. But her guns were too much. The volleys sent the devils scattering back into their woods—Leschi speaks Yakama, you understand. His mother was Yakama, and a young Yakama warrior had others there helping him. Do you know Nammakin, Eaton—if he belongs to Kamiakin?"

I did not recall the name.

"What is *xuun*?" said Nicholson. "*Yayk*?"

"Fish," I said.

"What kind? Where? When?"

"I cannot think."

Nicholson eyed my sunken-trembling cheeks and then looked knowingly at Narcisse and Taylor puffing up their countenances, tightening their jaws. "You cannot be squeamish about that squaw and her camp," he said. "She would never have been Christianized. She would never have planted seed or herded stock. Those are utopian dreams pursued by Indian lovers who make ignorant and impractical policies. I will never forget Narcissa Whitman who sacrificed herself ten years, leaving every comfort in New York to take in the half-breed children of lascivious squaws. 'Go ye into all the world and teach all the nations.'

"And you, Young Andrew, must never forget Miss Ward who the Indians killed south of Fort Boise, the bites on her cheeks, her beaten hands, a hot poker inside her female parts. You must never forget Missus King in her cabin outside Jacksonville, her womb sliced open, her fetus fed to hogs. The army would have prevented those murders if their troops had patrolled as bravely as the governor's."

"The fish are suckers," I said. "They run in the interior and Cascades well before the salmon."

"Where exactly?"

"Everywhere for everyone," I said.

And after tattoo and taps I lay in the dark in the barracks, listening to the stove tick dead, shivering in my buffalo robe and blanket, cowering from the eyes upon me—neither Christ's nor God's—not Narcissa's or Miss Ward's or Missus King's—but Lalooh's and the squaw's. For Lalooh had gazed at me two Januarys ago, fingering strange-shaped skull-bones of *xuun* and *yayk,* holding them in the glow of the cabin's hearth, brushing warmly against me, telling me why she had woven a new kind of fish trap. "This skull-bone is Blue Jay, see? This one is Cricket packing her child. This one, Raven. This one, Bear. This one, Coyote."

And so came the truth too tardy. If only I had remembered the voice of the one always in my heart, if only I had recalled her story of how the *xuun* and *yayk* had fallen from the sky, had shattered against the earth and had been formed again by the bones of many animals, so the *xuun* and *yayk* could remain in the creeks, and the Yakama could fend off late-winter starvation, catching them—if only Wool, Wells, Nicholson or the governor had considered how the Yakama had always gathered suckers in late February, we would have known where to find Kamiakin without advancing so recklessly our forces of persuasion.

The troops worked on the stables, a blockhouse, boats and rafts, and I paraded with Nicholson each morning, taking roll, compiling costs to submit to the War Department, and when the snow started to melt, we searched north again, riding through a stench of cattle and horse carcasses, passing live herds looking even hungrier than ourselves, their manes and tails chewed off—the results of horse cannibalism—of their owners wintering them in high hiding places rather than low valleys—and of finally abandoning them.

"More violations." Narcisse tore through packs left behind amid trails of unshod hooves. "The Palus and Wallawalla and Cayuse agreed to the governor's treaty, to stay here, and now they're fleeing to Nez Perce and trying to turn Lawyer into a killer too."

We reached the bare canyon wall again and went west along the rim and then down a gulch to the plain of the Snake, and we warmed ourselves during dinner, sitting in a dry draw out of a belting wind, and we gnawed wretched-moldy bacon—sucked it really, trying to keep our teeth in tact, spitting our scurvy blood.

And there amid a sand-blown rockslide grew Lalooh's *latitlatit*, the first Indian celery of the spring, an old Yakama cure for bloody gums. And I dug the sprouts with my knife, acting as if I had never seen them before, and I slipped them into my mouth and let their tender-peppery taste wallow secretly on my tongue. And I ate the sprouts greedily as I rode, feeling sure they were the same as those Lalooh had pulled from her waist-bag as she had laid a basket of suckers at the cabin's door last spring—I had named the fish correctly and had said the word I had known for wild celery, *lukš*. And Lalooh had darkened her gaze, had run out and rushed past a rockslide, pointing at *latitlatit*, and then we had climbed an outcrop to flatter leaves spread thinly on the rock, and she had reached beneath a crust of soil to rich-plump roots, saying, "Yes, this is *lukš*, Indian celery." And she had stood and pointed at a shaded slope, sunny slope, cliff-bottom, canyon-mouth, cliff-top, an arid bowl, a creek bank, mountainside, and she had named different Indian celeries in every place, her voice racing like Ma's whenever she talked about all the different peoples in Europe, how crucial it was to know them. And then Lalooh had quieted, gazing at all the spots again, and I had stood unable to repeat any of her names—only a sensitive young boy crossing his arms against a cold evening wind—a tag-along with his twenty-year-old brother, feeling only goose bumps, my favor and fancy rising hotly in my pants.

And Lalooh had spun and shot like a dust devil toward the creek, and I had never asked her how to say romance, love or sweetheart.

"You eating squaw weeds?" Narcisse drew beside me, eyeing my last handful.

"My mother says this plant stops gums from bleeding, just like limes on ships," I said.

"Your mother from Missouri? Now a webfoot from Brownsville? She lives in all that rain but knows cures from the Yakama desert?"

"We learned it emigrating."

"No, you're holding out. You learned it the same way I did, by watching Yakama squaws, and you make me think of where the Yakama will be. They'll be at the creeks around their old mission, catching those greasy little fish, gathering those greens they sing songs about."

"Not Kamiakin."

"Well, Nicholson won't send you alone to scout anymore. I'll go with you."

We rafted west across the Columbia and Yakama, found the old pastures up Ahtanum Creek recently grazed, no drying racks, no celery picked or dug, signs of warriors only, no squaws, and then we followed broad-beaten trails south to Status Creek.

Nicholson encamped us in a canyon, and Naricsse went up the creek bottoms, and I scouted across a couple ridges and smelled suckers and eels cooking, venison and beef, and her name came riding on the wind, reaching up into a hillside of oaks, shouted by a crier. *Lalooh!*

I crept down to the edge of a slope of rye grass, hundreds of horses browsing above a broad-winding creek-valley, a long string of lodges in *ha-haw*, the straight-spindly willow Yakama sometimes used for house-poles. And squaws walked beside the creek, singing, laughing, and Lalooh's cheeks arched smoothly through my spyglass, swelling grandly, bouncing with the steps of the aunt who carried her, a basket cap on Lalooh's head, designs on it like royal pyramids, fringes of dyed porcupine quills on a ceremonial shawl.

A hawk-nosed brave followed her, his gait a bandy-legged swagger, furs twined extravagantly in his hair. He thrust up his chin cockily, and I knew him as the warrior who had grabbed Dominique's reins outside Kamiakin's lodge during the treaty council. "Nammakin pays thirty horses!" shouted a crier, and Lalooh was lowered out of sight, and I turned weakly on my knees and groped up through the late-evening shade of the oaks, the crowns still bare, my mind suddenly muddy. Lalooh was with her groom in his lodge, their relations pouring shells and beads over their heads, and my feet were hurrying me from my despair, guiding themselves. I sneaked behind ridge-rock, racing, wanting to cry out, and I got to the butte overlooking our camp, and I felt hollow and sick, mute as if alkali parched my throat.

Two hundred forty of the governor's troops ate dust and hard-bread biscuits beneath me. And how many feasting warriors danced behind me? How many lodges stood? With what war chiefs? And what breastworks? I did not know. I had neglected my reconnaissance, and now Narcisse on his charcoal mare streaked through *ha-haw* bottoms, also returning.

I went down to Nicholson's tent, and Narcisse passed around an eagle-bone war whistle. "Eaton, did you ever see Kamiakin with this?"

"No," I said, I had not.

"I found cartridge papers too," said Narcisse. "There's a camp up a side creek, a huge cloud of dust."

"It looked like too many warriors to attack," I said.

Nicholson raised his eyebrows skeptically, "How many?"

"I couldn't get a vantage."

Nicholson blustered his breath down through his red-tangled beard, ordered weapons inspected, issued extra balls, powder, cartridge belts, and he posted guards on eminences all night and extra vigilance for signal fires.

Narcisse and I went out at dawn, leaving pickets below, scaling hills on mules, and he nodded at an open crown, and I thought maybe I had seen trails on the backside the evening before, so I nearly opened my palm, nearly slowed him, and then I drifted sideways, circling toward the backside, and he stopped, scanning with his spyglass, and Indians ran across the crown, shooting, and he crumpled, yanking reins, and my mule bucked, rearing, squealing, and I whipped it downhill, Narcisse's mule thudding behind me.

The pickets charged uphill, running past me, shooting, and I looked and saw Narcisse's mule still coming, Narcisse back on the ground between two big sage bushes, braves swarming toward him.

Narcisse raised himself on his elbow, and he fired his revolver, and a warrior pitched forward, a piece of his head flying backward, and *Bang!* Another spun away, hit square in the chest. *Bang!* A third fell, and Nammakin—Lalooh's groom—leapt from behind him, swinging a musket, and he drove the gun down against Narcisse, and he knelt with a knife, and I fired, and my shot sprayed short, and I pumped my ramrod, lying now behind my bleeding mule, the pickets spreading on both sides of me, also firing short, and I thought Lalooh would soon dance on my scalp, perhaps not even knowing it was mine.

More warriors rushed across the hill-crown, yelling, aiming muskets, drawing bowstrings, running directly down at us—they charged east toward the hill above camp and west down a butte toward the brush of the bottoms behind us—where a din erupted—shots, bugles, horses—Companies B,C,D, E galloping from camp.

Kamiakin waved his black flags atop the hill-crown, shouting, blowing a bone-whistle indeed, and clouds of arrows sang a terrible-pinging whine from rocks and bushes, and braves fired guns only when one of us revealed his position, shooting first, and all the while Nammakin lay flat behind Narcisse, showing only the wolf-ears of his war-cap, the barrel of Narcisse's breechloader.

And then Nammakin raised upon a knife the same parts that had sizzled upon the stove when Peopeomoxmox had died, and Phelps ran zigzags on my left, crouching compactly, staring fixedly at Naricsse, climbing, clawing at hammer and trigger, and *Thunk!* An arrow struck his shoulder, sending him sprawling on his buttocks, and he sat up, twisted the shaft, pulled out the head, stood, broke the arrow, tossed it away! And troops cheered anew, charging past me, muskets deafening, powder-clouds popping! Troops fired and knelt, reloading, and I bounded forward, aiming, shooting, kneeling in turn, and more troops charged, screaming, racing through dirt-clouds, stones and branch-bits flying, balls whistling, and Nammakin vanished marmot-like. He was suddenly gone amid stones and rocks, and Phelps and three others lifted Narcisse by the limbs, whisking him downhill, and I climbed behind a boulder, and I saw Nammakin shuffle behind sage near the hill-crown, and I feathered my rifle's trigger, and he fiddled with cap and breech-hole, and I thought of Lalooh in her wedding hat, and I eased off my trigger, and *Bang!* Phelps flew from Narcisse, hit in the back, and powder-smoke rose again from Nammakin's bush, but nothing else, no warrior.

I raced with others up the hill-crown, across it, down a ledge, down steps carved in rock and then to ropes hanging down a drop-off to a deep-winding crack, a passage two-warriors wide, bloody blankets, shirts and war caps riddled with bullet holes, ropes and withes used to drag away their wounded and dead.

"Down there!" cried Nicholson.

Kamiakin, Owhi, Skloom and Nammakin led mounted braves, galloping through an open-grassy bottoms hundreds of feet below, and I thought of Lalooh, the Dry Creek squaw again. "I'd stay out of there," I said. "We might ride right into hundreds more."

"I came to fight and kill Kamiakin, and I will fight and kill him," said Nicholson.

We returned to camp, not really knowing the Yakama's numbers, and Nicholson ordered our companies divided to hold all the bottoms and eminences around our canyon, and me to sit between him and Taylor, recording their accounts—*ten braves killed, three volunteers—Phelps, Narcisse and Brown from Cow Creek.*

An omen? I wondered. Some kind of all-knowing vengeance awaiting Taylor, Donaldson, Stewart and me? And all the others who had been at Dry Creek?

And then Donaldson strode hastily to us, removing his slouch hat, saluting to Nicholson and Taylor, his face sun-beaten and bone-jutted, his hair swept with rock-grit and desert-dust, scrunched down like dried-out straw, his eyes a desperate nut-brown, pinched between swollen lids. "The village is gone from the side creek, hardly a trace left behind. There's dust like they're going back to Ahtanum."

Nicholson glared at the kettle-clouds from mule meat boiling in a gruel of corn meal. "Where the hell is Major Wells? He's supposed to be here with a pack train and beeves! The Indians chose their ground! They outnumbered us, and we routed them like fleas! If we had Wells' regulars, we could have cut the whole of them to pieces! If we had fresh beef, we could finish them ourselves this week!"

I wanted none of my mule to eat, only to wash its blood from my skin, and I went over to the creek and dipped a bucket, and suckers shot sideways in thigh-deep rapids—school after school—plenty moist, chunky and flaky— plenty fatty—easy to catch and pack.

Wells' beeves were not needed, you see. We could eat the fish and follow Kamiakin north. Lalooh had brought a basketful to Jake and me nearly every day a year ago, had she not? But did not the treaty say *the exclusive right of taking fish in all the streams is secured to the said confederated tribes?*

I picked a ferny-leafed celery from a low-growing mat, and the hooves of a single mount pounded through the thump-and-slosh sounds of the creek. They beat a frantic gallop against stones and earth, racing downhill, getting louder. They thudded directly along the stream, and I stepped out of the *ha-haw*, and Dominique approached, whipping a pinto stallion, and this time I raised my hand, opened my fingers sure, and Dominique pulled up huffing, grimacing. "Why, Young Andrew, you're alive, by God, hello!" His gaze warmed and then flashed alarm. "The Cascades have been attacked, the blockhouse burned! Wells had to turn around! Indians had us holed up in the store four days, and a young lieutenant named Sheridan had to drive them off! The store happened to have army rifles and ammunition, otherwise—" Dominique pulled fingers up his forehead, indicating all whites would have been scalped, and suddenly he gaped at my face, flinching. He blanched, and we glanced sideways at camp, hammer-taps ringing throughout the canyon, saws grinding, Nicholson's carpenters building the coffins, hurrying to cap them before dusk.

"Narcisse?" said Dominique.

"Oh, let the Lord bury his deeds!" Dominique wrested his fists around reins, riding beside the coffin in the open wagon-bed. "Let the Lord bury his sins! Let Him take Narcisse upon a greater journey, for this is no longer a world for Narcisse!" Dominique looked ahead at the wagon's driver, lowered his voice, spoke sharply through his teeth. "It is no world for any half-breed, no, not these days! Narcisse tried to prove himself full-bred, white, American! He believed the governor and killed for him! This was Narcisse's lie, the one to snap his life in twain, to steal his honor!" Dominique thumbed his chest. "For I had no honor myself! I told and lived the lie and let it kill him! He deserved that beating, Andrew! I did an honest thing! I stopped Narcisse, but I made no account! I said nothing of it when we rode to the Blair ranch! I lied to myself instead! I told myself I made an account, that Narcisse understood, and I knew he did not! I know I do not understand now! Kill for those treaties? Speak for them? Cross the mountains for them? Die for them? There is too little truth in them, not any more than is inside a coyote—less, I say!" Dominique shook his head, his swamp-water eyes diving dismally. Tics pulsed in his long-elegant cheeks, froze, and his ruddy-brown skin creased with grief, and he gazed toward the world beyond the Cascades, his Babine wife waiting, and I felt my own misgivings, not boiling in my heart like his, but roiling inside my hands, actions not taken, deeds not done.

"The governor proposes," said Dominique. "The general proposes. But God disposes." We went up through oaks with the battalion, and he talked of Narcisse's boyhood, muttering swiftly, sometimes nearly breathlessly, and then we gained the pines, a level road, shadows, and he pulled out a Derringer, clicked through chambers, set caps, loaded cartridges. "Did you see who killed him? Who cut him?"

"Nicholson told you already," I said. "Nammakin cut him, but any warrior might have shot him. Do not blame yourself, Dominique."

"I do not! I still work for the governor, you see! He's been arresting half-breeds on the coast, and I've been translating his charges!"

Dominique shoved the Derringer beneath his frock into his waistcoat, and then he let his tears pour forth, hanging his head, and he did not wake from his misery until we reached the view of The Dalles—a veritable city now lay across the Columbia—a new fort, barracks and blockhouse, new tents, cabins and roads, assemblies of formal troops, a band in full dress, a new landing, the largest steamship I had ever seen above the Cascades, a sternwheeler flying Old Glory, the garrison flag, streamers.

Dominique rode past the coffin and beside the driver. He called out and dismounted. He threw the wagon's brake lever and led the wagon down a slope of jagged rocks and thin-coming grasses, and we got to the bank, and he shouted a flurry of French, Nicholson watching in consternation, trying to gather hundreds of anxious troops on shore downstream.

A salty-eyed boatman appeared, his crew seized the coffin, we tied it in a bateaux, and Dominique passed silver coins to French-Canadians, old company men in red-wool caps, and they knelt beside the pine box, chanting, synchronizing paddle-strokes through the squalling-banging waves.

We pulled beside the sternwheeler, and Dominique conferred with a lieutenant, and then he and I boarded the ship and climbed a stairway smelling of hot-sumptuous food. A guard led us into the texas, and a quartet of brass gazed up from the captain's table—the captain, the governor, Major Wells and General Wool, the latter looking twice as old the governor, easily two heads taller, his pate as bald as a seal's, shining broadly between cottony ear-tufts.

"Nicholson routed Kamiakin," announced Dominique. "The militia chased the Yakama toward Ahtanum, a total victory."

"Kamiakin surrendered his federation?" said the governor. "Was hanged?"

"No, I want you to see Narcisse," said Dominique.

The governor requested three more chairs, and the captain, three more servings.

"No, out here, please!" Dominique pushed out the door and waited by the rail of the hurricane deck, and the governor drew up on his left, Wool on his right, and the three men peered down at the coffin, Wells and the captain still coming. The governor groaned in grief. He leaned against Dominique, and Dominique reached into his waistcoat, and I tumbled hard, pushing Dominique forward, tangling his feet, and he fell, and I rolled and sat upon him, feeling Dominique's Derringer against my posterior, his hand squirming.

"I'm sorry!" I babbled intentionally. "I'm not used to ships!" I started to stand, felt Dominique reach again, fell on him again, and Wells and Wool grabbed me, and the governor leaned above Dominique, extending a hand, and I waited for the shot. "Narcisse was cut worse than Peopeomoxmox!" I cried.

"A barbarity," said Wool, his eyes solemn, his voice morose. "Whoever cuts a man like that deserves to be cut himself."

The general meant the words as solace, but Dominique slid an empty hand from his waistcoat and wiped his forehead uselessly, his color draining, his energy fatigued. He bowed to the four men, tucking his forearm against his waist. "I will dispatch my resignation." He went straightaway to the stairway and then reappeared walking weak-legged across the landing plank, and he got in the bateaux and shot with the boatmen and coffin through the sparkling spray of the evening sun, gorge-thunder booming, roaring all around us.

We watched silently after him, and then troops started to cross from the north bank, and I followed the officers into the cabin again.

The governor straightened his uniform, his West Point epaulets golden. He sat and spoke lustily to Wool. "You have seen Dominique's sorrow, and you still want to delay our retaliation? You know we have the worst country in the world to wait for summer operations. The Indians will take to the high country."

Wool nodded courteously, perusing his plate.

"I will send three hundred horsemen, two hundred pack animals, one hundred days of provisions next week," said the governor.

"Get your men home," said Wool. "Get them planting their fields. The Department of the Pacific has already ordered out of the field all territorial companies except the one which will escort you to Nez Perce."

"I can keep the Nez Perce out of the war without firing a shot, but there's not a single white home left in the interior, and Kamiakin's claiming victory."

"Wells will proceed north with at least eight companies. He will show off the army's forces, and the Yakama will regard them seriously."

"You think you'll talk with Kamiakin? Negotiate? He must surrender unconditionally first. He must be hanged just as his men were hanged at the Cascades."

"Wells will handle operations as the army sees fit."

"The army will clear the hostiles from Naches Pass, so the railroad can run another survey?"

"Not necessarily."

"Then you will simply prolong the war."

Wool's ear-tufts rose like an owl unduly disturbed, and I listened less, finishing my plate and then taking up Dominique's. I devoured venison steak, potatoes boiled with parsley, soft-doughy bread, steaming broth with sweet onions, steaming coffee, pooling-thick cream—consumed them shamelessly, quietly, half-hearing Wool and the governor, feeling each man's stare, knowing the rest of the troops would suffer standard mess, and Dominique was miffed at me.

But next I took up his son's plate, and I thought myself as fortunate as a magpie who flees the swoop of an eagle only to discover a whole dead horse while the rest of the flock argues over the carcass of a squirrel. I was alive after all, and I would see Jake soon. And Nicholson, Taylor, Stewart and Donaldson would be mustered out, and I would be free of any Dry Creek troops, and the governor would leave too.

I grabbed a piece of apple pie, and then Wool crooned, his watery-blue eyes sparkling as clearly as a mountain lake. "They say Dominique Purcell helped John McLoughlin plant the trees that bore the fruit for that pie, the first apples along the Columbia." Wool's ear-tufts inched backward like a healer selling a tonic at a medicine show. "You'll serve Major Wells again, Young Andrew? I would have asked Dominique, but he gave me no time. Tell me, will you accept the honor of filling your friend's footsteps? At least until he has had time to face his truth?"

And so the next morning I signed the army's papers again, and Wells issued me a regulation uniform, a breechloader, a two-day leave, and I loaded four months of militia pay and rode my gray toward Jake's claim, carrying the rifle on a shoulder strap, a new six-shooter in a saddle-horn holster, my bags of coin in new-polished saddlebags. I got halfway up Six-mile creek, and Jake's Indian boy shouted in Chinook from behind trees. *"Ka'hphow!"* Little brother! He led two ponies from the trees, one saddled, the other packed—the boy was part Wasco, part Klickitat, part white, but all Indian-looking, neither thirteen years nor ninety pounds yet. He had heard a rider coming and had hidden until he had recognized me, and now he glanced angrily uphill. He was leaving, not returning. *"Suk'wala?"* he asked. *"Le'bal? Po'lalie?"* A gun? Balls? Powder?

He a lifted a small bag of silver and a string of shell money from the coast, offering me both, and I shook my head *no, I would not trade*. I told him I would give him the things outright, but they would only bring him trouble. "I am dressed like this to talk with friendly Indians around The Dalles," I said. "They must give up their arms, or they will be jailed as hostile enemies."

The boy blinked as if hurt, and he mounted and rode away along the side-trail, veering from the creek, mumbling, and I never saw him again.

I went on up through the pines, listening for the sawmill, and I found it quiet, the blade and the steam engine cold. But boards stood stacked in wagons, and they were also piled on high ground all the way to the cabin, and I walked to the door, and it was latched with a new lock, and so I looked through a window—Jake had a store-bought mirror and hair brush on his table, a new featherbed and a pair of store-bought shoes on the floor—a *lady's* shoes.

I had my pay to secrete away, and I did not call out. I primed and loaded my rifle and stayed in timber, leading my gray around a clearing of downed trees, and then I picketed her and stepped into our old windfall, a giant fir which would not rot or burn for eons if left alone. I felt my way through the darkness inside the trunk and found the square Jake and I had cut in the bottom-side. Our safe was still buried, my key still fit, something white was piled inside— more shell money from the coast. I lit a candle, and the light licked up a wall of planks, and I un-wedged one, then another, and there was a coffin—no, a storage trunk so newly made the sap-smell and dust itched my nostrils.

The top lifted off, and I felt through bundles of root stems and ferns and grasses, stacks of coiled baskets, an otter cape, moccasins, a cedar-bark hat and dress, and then my gray nickered, and I hurried out, and she held her ears flat, looking across the clearing, sniffing—Jake led a beautiful sorrel mounted side-saddle by a woman dressed like a town belle.

I stepped into the open and shouted, "It is I, Andrew Eaton!"

Jake boasted to the woman. *"Ek'heh!" Brother-in-law.* The woman sat straight, and Jake grasped her waist, swinging her down, and her hat tumbled, her hair fell squaw-black, and she swiped it, and her brow looked flat, and I walked to them, feeling as put off as the Indian boy, and then the woman raised her hand, waiting for a kiss, gulping, looking at me wide-eyed, her lips about to quiver in fear, her face whitish but thick like a squaw's, her eyebrows plucked Indian-fashion.

I kissed her hand, though I was really not inclined. "An-dew," she said.

"Meet Missus Rachel Olivia Eaton," said Jake, "born Kankakee County, Illinois."

I did not think him serious.

"Muck'aluck," said Jake, and Missus Rachel led her sorrel downhill to cook a feast, her hoop skirt rustling awkwardly around logs, Jake beaming after her.

"Does Ma know?" I asked.

"Ma has a suitor of her own these days," said Jake.

"You cannot keep her here. You must burn all her Indian things."

"No, Andrew. I burned a few things, and she cried the same way Ma cried when Pa sold her books before we came west."

"Take her to Illinois, Jake. Everyone here will know what she is."

"Would you take Lalooh to Illinois?"

"Yes, even farther. Listen, Jake, your squaw doesn't look right, riding side-saddle. Every soldier in this country knows a coast Indian when they see one. They'll come up here and take her and kill her. They all know Leschi and other coast hostiles have flat heads and white-looking skin."

Jake eyed my uniform. "You have changed, brother—changed for the bad."

"Please, Jake, listen to me. Burn her things and take her to Illinois."

Jake looked up the mountain. "I found her about seven miles up. She was so desperate she was digging a pit to live in. You should see the trees up there—lumber enough to build every new town between here and the Walla Walla, and streams deep and fast enough to float the logs. She'll file a claim in her name as my wife. You should marry and file a claim too. When the trees go down, bunchgrass comes up. We'll graze herds much better here than we would have at Ahtanum."

"You and your squaw will not live that long."

"You're jealous, aren't you, brother? Did you ever find Lalooh?"

"You lost your boy, do you know? I saw him on the way up. You'll lose everything."

"Hog wash! You got no right to resent me so! She always says yes, she never says no! I'm keeping her, and you got no right to tell me different!"

I walked off. I sat by my gray and watched her browse until she was finished. I took her to the creek and let her drink, and then I descended a side-trail too, skirting the cabin, returning to the fort before dark.

3

General Wool commissioned all eight companies as he had promised, and we marched across the *Wahksums* again and encamped at Nicholson's canyon and found the Status thundering, flooding much of the ground where the militia had slept the month before, running too powerfully to dip buckets for suckers.

Major Wells and I climbed the hill where Narcisse had fallen, glassed the grassy bottoms below the backside, saw only a duck marsh. We retraced my old reconnaissance along the ridge-rock, glassed the old village site, saw Lalooh's wedding-stream so wide and the *ha-haw* so thick we surmised a great many war canoes might move invisibly below us.

The day we approached Ahtanum Ridge, warriors paraded distantly along the rim, and I led the force up a Yakama trail, and we descended toward the creek that had been flanked by a long-broad scar of near-frozen ash the month before. Now the valley shone green with new grass and green-fuzzy fringes of creek-shrubs, and pine sprouts glistened from a charred carpet of earth that stretched brightly black and smooth-looking. The sight caught me hard. I saw not a single lodge or cabin along the churning-sparkling creek—no cattle grazing, no fences, not a trace of horse herds or the trails Lalooh, Jake and I had known, or even of the chapel or the corral. Sidalia's garden showed itself a little, and I thought I saw where Lalooh and other squaws had fled down the bank before jumping in the Yakama. But the bends were underwater, and they did not look exactly right, and the air still smelled faintly of the fire.

The Indians who had paraded on the ridge had left no signs along Ahtanum Creek. Wells ordered all eight companies encamped. He placed pickets and cannon teams all around, and he sent me up-creek at dusk. "Wait until Arcturus is high in the east, and Capella drops in the west," he said. "Then the coyote will yip twice."

And so I went on foot past the last picket and beyond the burnt earth, well past the bank where the dance house had been, and I laid down my blanket in a cluster of brush not leafing out yet, and I sat huddling in a buffalo robe, watching Capella, and I thought of Ma in the dark of the plains, her breasts warm and dusty against my body, her eyes gazing at stars, her hand holding mine in a bucket of water, cooling the fingertips I had scorched when I had grabbed a buffalo chip from a fire.

Ma had beat dust from our wagon and clothes every evening our emigrant train had stopped in Kansas Territory. She had wiped dust from inside the kettle before supper and from outside it afterward. She was filmy and sweaty with dust, holding me, a wisp of corn-silk hair hanging dusty from her bonnet, her eyes deep and blue, always keeping track of me.

The dung stuck bubbling on my skin, and she picked it off and rubbed on bacon grease. She chattered softly and pointed me beyond our ring of wagons and the river smell and the Pawnee Village where Pa had gone. "Talking with squaw men," she said. "Brutes who surrender to filth." She buckled cold against me. Her breath caught with revilement. "Sinners."

She pointed me to the star pulsing just above the western horizon, shining brighter than all the others. "Capella," she said. "Neptune and his chariot and sea horses." She set her face, smiling and warming against me again. "Our train might make mountains of dust behind and ahead of us all day long, but it settles at night, and God calls us with the brightest star in the heavens. God calls us to make the brightest world on Earth, Andrew. He has placed the star out there to call America all the way to the sea where it sets. God calls you and me and Jacob and Pa. He calls Americans to be free in ways no people have ever known before. He calls us to work God's earth and grow His fruits in ways never so blessed as they will be in Oregon."

Capella pulsed at the edges of fir trees stubbornly tall and dark. It slipped behind the trees, and I stood above the river-brush, and I was sure I could not see it.

The coyote barked through the roar of the creek. I lit my tinder, fed it sticks of driftwood. Flames leaped brightly yellow, began to burn down. Brittle leaves crackled on rock.

"*Yuk'wa!*" Here! An Indian whispered in Chinook, then in Yakama. "*Wawáasway.*" Fishing pole. Wells' watchword. "*Aay.*" Hello. "*Táymu.*" News.

Suddenly Yakama John squatted before me, his gaunt-tawny face drawn tightly in the glow from coals. He was not of any Yakama band I had known, though Wells had said he had come into Fort Dalles after the Cascades massacre and had claimed Kamiakin would make slaves of any Indian who did not join the hostiles.

He laid the parched breastbone of a horse beside the coals and then drew a map on it with a stick of ashes.

The warriors had continued east on Ahtanum Ridge. They had passed un-noticed behind the new army of white soldiers. They would circle back ahead of us and join many bands who were gathering on the Naches, two or three days north.

And so one full year after I had stood beside the governor, speaking his words at the Walla Walla treaty, I rode with Major Wells along the south bank of the Naches while thousands of Yakama massed on the north side, the river between the whites and Indians screaming the melt of Rainier, the far-off ice fields draining a cloudy gray-grit into the blue-green froth, roaring down from the mountain where Kamiakin had been visited by a buffalo spirit and had learned his war song, Lalooh had once said. She had knelt in tules that day, and she had reached down into a mallard's nest, smiling at the hen squawking and flying a frantic circle, and then she had dropped eggs into the roll of her dress, her breasts no larger than her quarry, as smoothly curved, and she had caught me gazing at them, and she had tossed back her braids, laughing, chortling more deeply and heartily than any white girl, her eyes shining fondly at Rainier. "*Tahoma*," she had said, naming the mountain where a giant had been known to steal a beautiful squaw and hide her in his cave—a desire so real I still felt it.

More lodges rose every day on the slopes north of the Naches, and Wells glassed for Kamiakin, and I watched for Lalooh. There were more lines of dust on the horizon every day—more bands coming in from the root grounds in Kittitas Valley—more squaws, ponies and wagons loaded heavily with *lukš*—more squaws carrying serviceberry sticks for arrow-shafts and obsidian chips for points—more warriors with headdresses and painted faces and ponies—more campfires smoking with thick balls of dirty-black smoke—more evidence of Indians heating and forming more musket balls in molds.

"At least sixteen hundred warriors," said Wells. "And how many guns, Eaton?" The major knew I did not know. He was in rare humor, trying to smooth away our risk as he and I stepped into a pontoon boat. "How many warriors speak English, Eaton? How many squaws?"

He and I settled ourselves between two pairs of oarsmen, and *Boom!* A cannon-blank was fired, a colonel shoved the stern, and the boat jumped into the current, the oarsmen shouting commands, rowing to midstream, bolstered by lines strung to my gray and bay on the bank, troops flanking the horses, holding loaded rifles, standing in full dress.

Wells held a white flag, kneeling, and I called out in Yakama. "I am with a great war chief of the Great Father's army! Major Wells has come all the way from Washington City to talk with Kamiakin, Owhi, Skloom, Teias! Major Wells will talk with those who have peace in their hearts! He wants no more whites on Yakama land! He invites the Yakama to lay down arms! He invites the Yakama to feast, smoke and talk peace!"

Warriors stepped out from behind rocks and trees, drawing bows, cocking muskets and pistols, and I shouted the message again, watching an older brave who reclined upon the boulder at water's edge, glowering into the river. He had sat there every day since our command had arrived, and now he seemed to ignore our boat. "He Who Watches For Salmon!" I called. "Will you find Lalooh, daughter of Sogesehi, She Who Speaks English? Will you send a crier through Kamiakin's camp?"

The brave cupped his hands around a knee, stretching his spine luxuriously, and Nammakin rose from a boulder beside him, holding a painted pole with a white scalp dangling from a charcoal-colored horsetail. He glared at Wells, at the white flag snapping in the wind, at the gulp moving down through my throat. He called in English, "I am Nammakin, son of Lolowet, nephew of Owhi! I killed Narcisse Purcell at Status Creek!" He pumped the scalp and grinned triumphantly. "I learned the white tongue from Lalooh!"

"This is Andrew Eaton, my interpreter!" called Wells. "Would you ask him anything in your own language?"

Nammakin called in Yakama to me, "You are the woman who learned Yakama from Lalooh? The one who used our words against us?"

I remained mute, and Wells looked at me, waiting.

"He said I told lies for the governor at Walla Walla," I said.

"I see," said Wells.

Nammakin shook Narcisse's scalp at the major's flag of truce. "Our Words Against Us, Bloody Beard and Narcisse Purcell spoke peace with Peopeomoxmox in such a way!"

He turned and walked away between trees, a hoard of braves trailing after him, the salmon brave still reclining, refusing to raise his stare from the rapids.

And two days later Wells and I rode the south bank, and squaws walked with their back-bundles along the north bank, and Lalooh was among them, carrying a pile of serviceberry sticks higher than her head, wider than her shoulders, her pretty-broad cheeks hard-set, her breasts so big against her buckskins I wondered if she were starting with child. And she felt my stare, turning, and she pitched down, branches flying from her pack, spilling over her head, and the salmon brave rose angry-faced from his boulder, and he shouted at her, the Naches drowning out all his meaning but the meanness of his voice. Lalooh rose to her knees, tugging her brow-strap, her pack straight, and the brave grabbed a fistful of branches and swung them, knocking off her cap. He whipped her shoulders. He flailed her back and legs, cursing her. He pointed his sticks one-handed, directing her, and she shed her pack and picked up loose sticks while other squaws veered away, hurrying past her, and then she arranged sticks, and the brave yelled on, beating her shoulders, his branches whipping like rods, and he tossed them on her load, still waving and yelling, and she hoisted her bundle and went off, hiding her face, leaning heavily, fleeing unevenly, and the brave sauntered to his rock again, sat boastfully, grinned at us—a sorry-looking needle musket propped against his boulder, probably too old to shoot across the river—my breechloader could have reached his smile readily—but we had orders to hold our fire unless the enemy threatened our lives—so I rode on with Wells, acting as if I paid Lalooh no mind, for everyone knew a brave beating a squaw meant no more than a mosquito stinging a cheek.

"Do you know her?" Wells studied my face. "Is she from Kamiakin's band?"

I shook my head, feeling too stingy-hearted to say—troops all around us were soaked with sweat, swinging bill hooks, slashing willows, and the catkin-fluff and blossom-fragrance swirled and hung and blew in the air as the men wove the stems into frames of scrub-cottonwood, making gabions, filling them with dirt and stone, piling them in front of trenches, laying on sod before the artillerymen rolled up the howitzers, mounting them on the breastworks.

We rode to Wells' tent, and I wrote dispatches all afternoon, and in the evening I went over to the fiddle-playing, sat on the bank, joined the privates who eyed squaws, and I glassed those who limped, and I got to sulking, fretting, and the privates whispered among themselves, smirking about Young Andrew who had it so easy.

And later I lay hot on my blanket beneath a sheet of canvas, smelling the willow-fragrance as thickly as boiling sap, as penetrating as lilacs. I knew I still told myself lies about last spring, still dreamed something gone. Lalooh had wanted to live as an Indian, not a white, though I would not have worked her as a pack animal in a white marriage, would not have allowed any man to beat and berate her, no matter the whereabouts of Nammakin or the rage of any other brave.

Very early the next morning—before mama quails popped their high-little cries in the brush, while coyotes still yipped—I met Yakama John, and he whispered his intelligence, and I stopped him before he skittered soundlessly away. *Did he know Lalooh from Kamiakin's band? And the fisherman who beat her? If she was with child? If she needed laudanum from the army?* He laughed to himself—insulted the medicine man might be insufficient, aghast I should worry about a squaw.

He left, and I memorized his message—*Yesterday Owhi and Skloom had dismissed Kamiakin as a chief only by marriage, not blooded like themselves, and they had denounced his call for more warriors to fight and defeat the whites.*

I went in and reported to Wells and then rode back with him as the dawn-sun sent a glittering yellow sheet racing up the snow-cap of Rainier. We hid our horses in sage, and we crawled onto a rock-cliff at the mouth of a creek, spy-glassed across the Naches, and there slept the chief of the federation, lying in a gulch two miles above any other Indian, his back and blanket twisted away from their encampment, his big hands clasped beneath his big-cut chin, the rippled cords of his calf muscles outside his covering, no whiskey bottle or cup anywhere, the sunrise lighting up rabbitbrush, slanting a shadow across the chief's rump.

Wells put away his glass. He squinched his eyes in disbelief, curled his lips smugly, and we left Kamiakin sleeping in isolation, thinking John's dawn-words had been as solid as the gold coins I had put in his hand.

We rode back toward Wells' tent, intending to commiserate with colonels, eyeing what we could of the Indian camps. We rode directly opposite the Indian council grounds and found blue-shirts crowding our breastworks, intently watching a lone brave clinging to the mane of a horse swimming the river, the Naches sweeping the two swiftly toward the stronger-higher Yakama. The brave gained an island mostly submerged, and the horse paused amid willows, its dappled snout snorting through snapping-spraying branch-tops. Both mount and brave labored, the brave's hawk-nose swelling, the swagger of his chin unmistakable.

Nammakin and his horse kicked fully into the current again, Nammakin staying downriver, pressing his chest forcibly against the horse, his body sometimes whipping like a snake, and then he landed and dismounted, and troops circled him, and Wells and I rode up, and he stood unarmed, breechclout dripping, chin held unmercifully high.

"Owhi wants peace," he said in English. "Skloom wants peace. But I am a warrior like Kamiakin. I do not want peace. I would rather die, and that is why I am here. If I am killed, Owhi and Skloom will fight on, and you whites will be driven away. If I live, Owhi and Skloom will fight no more. Now you know the object of my coming. I am waiting."

"Where is Kamiakin?" asked Wells. "Is he afraid to swim the river himself?"

"Kamiakin went off to dream by himself, made sick by Owhi's talk. He will not come in and trade our land for promises from white men. But I am waiting. If you do not kill me, I am ashamed."

Gun-hammers clicked behind us, boots shuffled nearer Nammakin, and shackles clinked, but Wells gave no orders, peering stoically at the brave.

"No, you are not ashamed," said Wells. "You are a true-blood chief, and we will not kill you yet, Nammakin. We will not seize you here as cowards seized Peopeomoxmox on the Touchet. I will give you instead another message to take to Owhi, Skloom and the other chiefs—if they want peace, let it be peace. If they want war, let it be war. They must see I have here cannons and troops enough to wipe them from the face of the earth. They must know the disasters of fighting on—all their warriors killed, or driven away never to return, and their women and children starving to death. They must also know I pity their condition, and I will make them happy if they comply with my demands."

Nammakin grabbed a braided buffalo-hair bridle and looped and tied the slack around his waist. He spoke not a word to his mount, nor another to us. He and his piebald swam across the current again, and he got out and stood on the bank, the wind blustering now, blowing a snowstorm of cottonwood seeds and willow-fluff above the Naches, the puffballs white and airy, their insides twinkling, retaining a bright glow of the desert sun, plastering and clinging to his wet-glistening muscle.

One hundred warriors arrived at our bank the next day, Owhi rising from a canoe in his war costume, Lalooh behind him wearing a beaded dress whitened beautifully with clay, her shoulder slumping stiffly, her cheeks and chin suddenly as haughty-looking as her husband's, though Nammakin wasn't with the peace party.

Wells and his colonels and I waited beneath an arbor, and Lalooh approached beside Owhi, refusing to meet my glance, the only squaw with the chief, small but impetuous-looking beside him—Owhi sauntered toward us sternly, his bearing sturdy and Roman, his brow as imposing as a cliff-face, his hair graying, his skin wrinkled deeply around his eyes. He stopped a few feet away and stared ceaselessly at Wells, and Lalooh gazed fixedly at the ground as if she loathed to look at us.

Owhi spoke, and she translated, "We do not need your young one here. We remember him from Walla Walla when he spoke like a dog drooling foam."

"Who is your interpreter?" asked Wells.

"Lalooh, wife of Nammakin."

"Her English sounds able enough."

Owhi breathed deeply, slowly, and he looked at the white fluff still blowing from cottonwood crowns.

"These seeds are like my people," translated Lalooh. "They need only water and land enough, and they will grow. They can wash downriver, and they will grow. They can blow to a new valley, and they will grow. But if too much blood drenches them, they will collapse upon themselves, and they will sink and choke and shrivel."

Lalooh's breasts swelled amply as she spoke. She wore no pregnancy belt. Her stomach stretched flatly, and her chin arched as if her marriage and the English I had taught her had turned her into royalty, no matter who beat her.

"I am glad of this day," said Wells.

"The treaty is the cause of all the blood between us," translated Lalooh. "The treaty pulled the Indians from their homes. It tore them apart like the wind tears hairs of silk from these seed-balls. It poured poison on every silk-hair. It drenched each silk-hair with lies. It weighed down every silk-hair, so they would not sail freely. It put some seeds where they would have no water. It put others where they would have no sun. It made sure the whites would settle on our lands, and their wagons and trains would trample us into the earth."

"The bloody shirt shall now be washed, not a spot left on it," said Wells. "Now you can take care of your people, and I will take care of mine."

"It seems wherever I look, I see blood," said Owhi. "Wherever I breathe and drink, I taste blood. As the sun now shines, so my heart feels bright for peace."

"We will build a bridge," said Wells, "and when we finish it, you will have five days to surrender everything you have stolen or captured from whites. You must bring every chief in your camp over here to feast. Every chief must agree, and then we will keep away miners and settlers while you fish."

We sat upon a blanket to smoke, and Lalooh tucked her legs in a kind of genteel deference beneath her knees, bowing her head so near me I smelled the mashed leaves of some Indian celery I could not name, a poultice beneath her dress, and I spied the dullness in her eyes, a continuing refusal to look at me, her mood a dreadful daze that kept a somber grip on her even as the Indians launched canoes back into the Naches.

Lalooh did not paddle as they returned. Her mother and aunts met her, and they hurried away from Owhi and climbed toward a veil of dust hanging above a hot shimmer of bare-beaten earth and chalky sage—Kamiakin's old circle had been entirely vacated—everything was gone—lodges, horses, cattle—and a good many Yakama warriors too.

To where? North to the people of Kamiakin's father, the Palus? To incite the Spokane and the Okanogan in Canada? Or east to incite the Nez Perce? Or west to the foothills to attack our timber crews? Or to Naches Pass to harass supply trains? Or to Puget Sound to recruit from Leschi's bands? Or to the Columbia to attack the Cascades again?

And who knew? The sad little squaw who spoke English so spitefully? Nammakin's wife?

I woke and rose in the dark, reviewing Wells' questions as the glow of the forge pulsed across our encampment, casting red-and-yellow ghost-shapes across uncountable tents and men slumbering openly between robes and India rubber blankets, the troops still two hours from reveille, the blacksmiths already heating iron for bridge-anchors. I walked beneath Cygnus and the Milky Way, moving through the stenches from pack-cover tents propped up by muskets and poles, smells of semen and piss, unwashed flesh, sweat-drenched wool, diarrhea, flatulence—of sour-breathed coughs heralding consumption and pneumonia, some troops muttering and jabbering in dream, others moaning, snoring, wheezing. The stables and corrals stank of warm-baked earth, dung, sweaty leather; the slaughterhouse, of drying blood, fear and rotten innards.

I skirted an immense plain of bunchgrass, the kind of vast valley which inspired dreams of cattle empires, and then I entered the river-brush and proceeded a couple miles, and I lay waiting for John, and steps padded across twigs and sand, and I crouched behind a shrub, opening my holster, and two braves slowed before the shrub, looking skinnier than John, peering down, pointing muskets, and I rose, whispering in Yakama, and the taller one whispered in Salish, and I understood only, "Quiltenenock," "Skistymay." I spoke my name, and another warrior catapulted between them, butting me, knocking me through branches. Hands clawed at my throat, and I bucked, grabbing hair, a braid, and was shoved deeper into stems, pounded by fists, and a knife rose, Lalooh, and I rolled, shoving her shoulder, and she shrieked, and I bucked again, and she flew against Quiltenenock, and he caught her, clasping her mouth roughly, wanting her quiet—the same demand I received from Skistymay, who was planting a foot painfully upon my chest, holding a musket an inch from my mouth.

I lay with my hands sprawled, and Skistymay leaned nearer, taking my pistol, and then he eased up with his foot.

"He is one from Dry Creek," said Lalooh, and the foot upon me stiffened again, and Skistymay seemed to straighten in disgust, and then he loomed blue above me, the sky paling overhead, his dark eyes roaming with painstaking slowness, gawking at my every loathsome feature.

He raised his musket as if to smash my skull, and Quiltenenock caught the barrel—the Sinkiuse chief was painted blue like Skistymay, war feathers dangling from his hair, grizzly and wolf claws from his neck—I hated him thoroughly for a moment—he had allowed me life, and I wished myself dead.

Lalooh translated for him, glaring as if she were sorry she had failed with her knife. "We did not kill John. Others saw him leave you yesterday. We came instead to show the major a letter from Father Sidalia. The black robe says the Sinkiuse are friends to whites, and they have fished at their home since before the whites."

"Do not be angry," I said, desperate to appease Lalooh. "The major thinks the Sinkiuse deserve their land. He would let all the Indians alone between the Cascade Mountains and the Columbia."

Quiltenenock returned my pistol, and I signed for the Sinkiuse to empty their guns, and they did, and I knew I had better impress them. I led them past the cavalry drilling and sharpshooters practicing, the magazine and hundreds of tents, and then Wells joined us, and we went up to the breastworks and cannons and looked down at the freshly cut timber already lying snugly on the bank, smoothed over with sand and pebbles into a landing for three deck-sections already fitted and lashed atop a dozen pontoons, cables vibrating down into rapids, holding firmly. "Five days," I said, reiterating the terms Wells had offered Owhi. I pointed to where the bridge would land across the river, and Lalooh chortled deeply, so briefly I doubted the laugh. But Quiltenenock brightened his eyes fiercely. Spring salmon had begun to run in earnest, bumping snouts against pontoons, massing as great-gray hulks, flicking tails, holding themselves effortlessly against the current, also shooting through bridge-gaps, hurling themselves above rapids. But no Indians were fishing.

There were no weirs. No spearing. No netting or clubbing. No scaffolds.

Squaws collapsed lodges across the river, saddled mounts, loaded bags, and Lalooh named creeks, traditional fisheries of different bands, better harvest-places. "Owhi says you must wait at least ten days, not five," she said. "Otherwise our people will not get enough fish, and we will starve this winter."

"Owhi has gone?" said Wells. "And where is Nammakin? And Kamiakin?"

Lalooh grew stony.

"Your people will rendezvous somewhere."

"The Council of Braves would not say," said Lalooh. "If they had, my fate would be the same as Yakama John's."

Wells grew stony too, and suddenly a fish thumped into a boat above the bridge, and a blue-shirt staggered up, wrestling a sixty-pound buck, the salmon winning, slapping against a bone-jutted figure. The man fell against an oar, his nut-brown eyes amused but also alarmed—Donaldson? Here in Wells' army?

Quiltenenock passed his letter, and Wells read it and ordered us hastily from the breastworks and council arbor, away from any view of the grand departure, and we proceeded to his tent and convened beneath awnings, smoking and eating with his colonels. "I am glad the Sinkiuse are not here to fight," said Wells. "If I ever get hold of another Indian who stirs up trouble, he shall surely die."

"Kamiakin is not our chief," said Quiltenenock, Lalooh translating. "Skloom and Owhi are not. We did not sign the treaty. We want only to stay on our lands and keep the chick-chick wagon away from our home. If the chick-chick tries to cross the Columbia, it will crash and kill our fish. If it tries to cross the mountains, it will crash and scare our game and our spirits. If it comes, it will only bring whites, their diseases, their greed for our land."

"The railroad will come," said Wells.

"Three years ago the governor's man, a red beard, came with his red and white rods and measuring chains. He said the same as you, the chick-chick will come. But we showed him the footprints on the rocks on our banks, those made by the first Indians. We told him, no, his gifts were no good." Quiltenenock looked at Wells. "But you and I are friends." He looked at Skistymay. "After the treaty Looking Glass gave Kamiakin a war horse, a buckskin shirt and leggings of cougars' teeth, a new rifle and six-shooter, a war cap of eagle plumes reaching to the ground. He said to Kamiakin, 'Present these things to the bravest man you know.' And Kamiakin gave them to Skistymay, yet Skistymay has stayed home during the war. He has killed no whites."

"Yes, return to your home and fish," said Wells. "Make no trouble with the whites, and I will be your friend."

"The treaty will be changed," said Quiltenenock.

"No, not yet," said Wells. "I cannot."

"What will the governor say?"

"The governor is not here."

"But he is on his way. He left Olympia with two hundred soldiers and one hundred pack animals. He crossed the snow of Naches Pass. He is three days away."

Wells gripped the arms of his field chair, nearly bucking his spine, and his sun-reddened skin wriggled around his bullet-eyes, preventing them from popping open at his colonels—the small band of Sinkiuse had better intelligence than the entire Pacific army, and Lalooh, more composure than the major. She, not I, continued to translate, and she sat only in plain buckskins, no ceremonial hat or face paint or beads, eyes patient, a calm sweat on her cheeks, a quiet droop to her damaged shoulder, a calm breath in her heart, and a secret resurgence in mine, a hope I could somehow speak into her silence and win her forgiveness.

"What does the major say?" She spoke for Quiltenenock. "Shall we wait for the governor?"

"Has the governor met any resistance since leaving Olympia?"

"No."

"Has he encountered Kamiakin or Owhi or Skloom?"

"No."

"Has his militia fought or killed any hostiles yet?"

"No."

"Then go swiftly," said Wells. "With great caution."

The afternoon the bridge was finished, a procession of officers crossed it, and Dominique Purcell marched beside me, stepping gingerly but firmly, working for the governor once again, his cheeks still grief-creased, his nose and chin newly angled, gaunt, his torso hanging slackly from his shoulders as if

Narcisse's death had worn away his flesh as incorrigibly as spawning eats and wastes a salmon. His eyes remained deliberately inquisitive, but they grew murky, slow and catty as the governor anguished, tensing his hard-little body beside Wells, pausing before an encampment grounds now entirely vacant of Indians.

"Gone," grumbled the governor. "Scot-free. I despise very much your subservience to expediency rather than principle, Major Wells. And so does every honorable man—it is better to die in a just cause than to live by abandoning it."

"One can also abandon a cause by a needless bullet or starvation or blindness," said Wells.

"You forget the blind cannot see, and this life only prepares us for the next, His greatest glory," said the governor. "You forget that Owhi, Teias, Kamiakin and Nammakin must hang. You forget Skistymay has been seen wearing the scalps of miners."

Dominique loomed motionlessly, standing at attention as meticulously as I, and then a roar erupted, knocks and splashes and shouts, and the governor spun and sprinted to the landing—a pandemonium of blue-shirts swayed and rocked in panic on the pontoon bridge.

Two men ran toward us, the deck pitched, and each flew to either side, sprawling arms, tumbling into the Naches. Others lay across the deck, clinging to rails. Some swam above and below the bridge, and others tread water, reaching beneath bouncing pontoons. Others waded clinging to anchor cables, feeling beneath the surface with hands and feet.

A sergeant at the south end of the bridge raised a bullhorn, and it flew from him as he reeled backward, the deck heaving again, more men rolling and falling as if from an earthquake.

The governor raised his pistol—Wells' troops had failed to move properly on the bridge. The shot silenced their din. The troops stared, and the governor barked left, right, and men parted, glancing nervously at rapids, stepping reluctantly in line, sheepishly to either side. "Route step only!" The governor watched as the deck and pontoons grew level, and then he demonstrated the step, glaring at Wells' bridge-sentries. He eyed a root-wad pressing against an anchor cable upriver, its trunk jammed beneath the bridge. He eyed eddies downriver, and he saw blood, everyone said later.

He looked directly at his feet and inserted his saber beneath a lashing and cut it. He pried up a rail and deck planks, tossed them aside and glared at Wells' sentries again, daring them to move falsely. He knelt and pulled up the top of a body by the armpits, its blue-sleeved arms dripping lifelessly beside his hips, and then he clutched, unable to pull the body any farther. He nodded, and three soldiers hurried over, the deck bounced, the tree-trunk slammed the underside, the man's arms flopped wildly. But the man no longer felt any pain—the soldiers pushed their feet through the hole, depressing the trunk, and the governor slid Donaldson completely onto the deck, his sandy hair washed scarlet, his forehead crushed, his nose and mouth mostly gone, his belt sunk through his uniform, his waist linked to his legs only by shreds, a sodden-matted mess of sunken blue flannel and unrecognizable pieces.

And one can abandon the cause by negligence and incompetence, by the failure to administer discipline in step and an adequate crew to clear debris.

The governor did not speak these words, but his posture declared them as he rose from Donaldson, and they loomed inside Wells' voice the next day as he dictated letters to Donaldson's parents and Wool.

"Private Donaldson did not die from any lack of procedure," I said.

Wells nodded absently, the sun blazing against his tent's roof, his bullet-eyes pale and weak, eyebrows twitching with hair so scant it seemed permanently bleached by the desert.

"Donaldson was struck asunder," I said.

Wells tapped his pipe upon his desk and grasped it as if to refill it, and I spoke of Dry Creek, and he let the stem lie. I spoke every detail. "I helped carry her in," I said, finishing. "Her thighs were sopping with blood, and I held the pistol to her head."

Wells poured two cups of whiskey, placed one before me, drank, let his whiskey wallow and sink slowly.

"Do you know Carlisle?" he asked. "His four stages of man? The savage hunter? Shepherd? Tiller of the soil? And finally the citizen who understands and works with all spheres of civilization? Savage met savage there at Dry Creek. You had two flocks at war, and neither had a shepherd.

"Donaldson has met his judgment not here in this world, but from One in another world I cannot fathom. But you have not met yours yet, Andrew. You might redeem yourself and thousands of savages into the next century. You might learn more of their languages and tell the Indians why they must change. Or you might go east and learn law and return to this country and practice it.

"I cannot grant you leave to see a priest or reverend. But experience is the best of instructors during war. You will never reconcile all the acts and orders committed by volunteer militia and their impromptu commanders. The best you can do is to never join them again."

Wells reached down to his desk and lifted a dispatch from the governor, who had encamped separately across the Naches. He read it aloud: "*My authority as the highest federal official in the Territory is derived from the same source as the Major and General commanding the Pacific Division. I am commissioned by the President, and I act under authority of the laws of Congress. Thus I will not remain here and allow the Indians to compile stores for a winter campaign. My two hundred horsemen will, with the cooperation of a Nez Perce auxiliary and three companies of regular troops from the Pacific Division, drive the enemy out of their fisheries and across the Columbia. We will restrict the enemy to the country north of the Snake and will secure both the Wallawalla and Yakama country before emigrants arrive in the fall.*"

Wells dictated his reply: "*Though the Walla Walla treaty remains un-ratified, you must obey it, for you risk fewer lives respecting its boundaries than by violating them. Owhi is due to return in four days, and we will send a message through him to call in Quiltenenock to discuss the Sinkiuse territory and fishery, as neither are necessary to whites, nor to the Yakama. I deny any requisition for any operation north. I will not muster in any Nez Perce to go north, due to the violation of the treaty and their alliances with the Spokane and Okanogan there.*"

Wells folded his refusal ceremoniously, and I carried it through camp and across the bridge as the sun slipped behind Rainier, and gilded rays rose behind the peak, and the chill of the heights wafted down, feeling first like the breath of the Lord, a release from the heat, then like the old-winter judgment again, the cold air of the snowy bottoms, the gaze of the pregnant squaw as she looked up from her pile of branches.

A sentry escorted me through guards and up a butte—Dominique and the governor sat atop the crest, stretching their legs on buffalo robes left behind by Indians, drinking whiskey too.

The governor's big-hazel eyes burned beneath his protruding brow like angry flames in the twilight. "Owhi will not come in," he said. "None of his Indians will."

"The major let the enemy escape," said Dominique. "He built a bridge to nowhere, and he made the drowning a certainty, opening it too soon."

"No," I said. "The major proposes. The governor proposes. But God disposes."

I told them of Dry Creek, every detail I dared again. I listed the perpetrators now dead, and the governor drained a woven-hemp cup, his spine perfectly upright in the dark. "Lieutenant-major Taylor gave you the order to hold the pistol?"

"Yes sir."

"Then I fear your vanity has erred you, Andrew," he said. "When I left Olympia, Lieutenant-major Taylor and Private Stewart were well at Fort Steilacoom, and no savage had yet claimed the great temptation of Major Nicholson's red-haired scalp. You see, you have assumed only what the Great Being can know. Though a priest might forgive you, I trust a reverend would tell you so.

"I wish you would act a Puritan, Andrew—as a Patriot who fears the wrath of God and seizes the helm of leadership, so our land might rid herself of centuries of sin and anarchy. I wish you had marched with General Scott from Veracruz to Mexico City. The Mexicans were subdued, but no one violated them. The Mexicans showed hope of reform, you see. Cortez and the Spaniards had at least begun to shine the Light there, even if their bishops and cardinals clouded the word of Christ. But the natives here cannot learn Christ. Quiltenenock will not come in, and Skistymay will not. In 'fifty-three the Sinkiuse showed my man McClellan a lava hole and called it the first footprint in the world. They still believe it. They worship demons. They kill their medicine men for failing to cure incurable fevers. They crown their princes with wanton polygamy and adultery, and they smell devils inside the bellies of locomotives. They would pray away the railroad if they could. They would chant it and dance it away."

Dominique lay supine upon the dark fur of a buffalo robe, blowing a sigh, clearing the air, and the governor rose, grasped my hand, bowed good night. He limped slightly, favoring his good leg into the blackness of the night, and then his gait smoothed toward the lanterns and the guards at his tent, and I sat again beside Dominique, knowing he had helped feed both Protestant missionaries and Catholic priests during his early days at Fort Walla Walla.

"Why are you here?" I whispered.

"The governor offered me an Indian agency once the treaty is firm," said Dominique. "Probably the Yakama reservation."

"But that is not why."

"No, my friend, it is not."

He lay in the dark, his ankles limply locked beneath buffalo fur, his arms folded slackly across his white-silk blouse. "Do not lie," he said. "Do not tell me weak is strong and wobbly is solid. Tell me, did the Dry Creek squaw give you the intelligence you wanted?"

"Yes."

"How?"

"Narcisse was there, the last man with her, using a stick."

Dominique gulped audibly. He stared upward a long time, and I did know if he tried to stare through the infinite-cloudy haze to heaven or feel down into some dark hole inside himself. He sat up and grasped my thigh. "Father Sidalia was at The Dalles, and I told him about the hurricane deck, and he said he had always believed in you, and you finally had found Christ. Yet now you say you and Narcisse allowed yourselves to—" He shook his head, unable to go on. He reached down and raised from the darkness of a buffalo fur a dark bag, beads glowing from it like animal eyes in the night. "The treaty is still no good, but now I see what the governor has seen all along. Red man cannot live with white." He pulled a ball of dogbane twine from the bag. "Some squaw left this behind—*itita'mat*. It unravels at least forty feet. It might record generations before Christ—long enough anyway. The red man can step aside now."

"Will you sell this?"

"No, it is yours! I owe it to you!"

Dominique placed the ball in my hand, and I felt through the twine for my crooked hairs, any indication of Lalooh. "Tell the truth," I said. "Do not say weak is strong and wobbly is solid. Are you here to exterminate?"

"I cannot say. I only know I must see Nammakin who cut my son. I do not know if I will kill him or be his agent or interpret his confession or what."

"Nammakin speaks English already. He learned it from his wife Lalooh."

"Your pretty little squaw?"

"Yes, I must see her as you must see her husband."

"Ah, you are like me!" cried Dominique. "You do not seek anything real anymore, but you might catch it anyway! Come over to us, Andrew! Since we cannot go north, we will go south to find the old hideout where Kamiakin formed his federation, and maybe some Yakama wives will be there, gathering camas or heating iron for hostiles intent upon exterminating *us*."

The Naches dropped, pontoons rested on rock, the salmon and the willow and cottonwood seeds waned. The mercury in Wells' thermometer rose to one hundred ten, and cracks opened in the empty Indian grounds, and long-tongued lizards, cannibal ants, rattlers, mice and dung beetles crawled out. Owhi did not come in. Nor Skloom nor any other chief.

I went with the governor down the Naches and Yakama valleys, and we boated across the Columbia and rode up the Walla Walla again, Lalooh's *itita'mat* in one of my saddlebags, my crooked hairs on it, a new dentalium bead for her wedding, and I figured I would see her again, would return the ball no matter the river to cross, would stand before her people as Nammakin had stood before mine. *I am Andrew Eaton, son of Samuel and Alicia Eaton of Beaufort, Illinois, and I was not raised to kill, mutilate, violate or shirk from fear. I learned Yakama from Lalooh, daughter of Sogesehi, and I made bad words to Kamiakin at Walla Walla, and I did not speak enough about Agent McKalb and Macis. I aimed high at the battle of Ahtanum, so Lalooh could escape, and I watched bad men kill innocent chiefs on the Touchet, and I felt too afraid to object. I took orders from bad men at Dry Creek, but I did not climb upon the squaw as others did, yet I was afraid, and I held a pistol to her head, and I made it so. I might have shot Lalooh's husband twice at Status Creek, but I did not pull the trigger, and Nammakin shot Sergeant Phelps. I have sinned both my people and yours, but I am no longer afraid. You and your chiefs can take me, and I will make a blood payment to the relatives at Dry Creek. I will make a horse or gold payment, or you may whip, deface or kill me. I am waiting.*

"Nammakin might fall, and she might be captured," said Dominique. "You might have her released and give her a life of comfort."

The morning we turned south up Mill Creek, Wells was already many days north, searching in high country for the fisheries Lalooh had named—likely places to find Owhi and her people, but I supposed they would not be found so easily anymore.

We proceeded past wheat rustling gold and ripe with no one to harvest it, past cabins and frame houses whistling emptily. We approached the old council grounds, and Nez Perce lodges were strung beside the creek again, and a long line of mounted warriors waited for us, wearing festive regalia. They fired revolvers, welcoming us, and Pretty Jim—Lawyer's best scout—stood high in his stirrups, waving Old Glory. He instigated a *hip-hip-hurrah* in English, flanked by two officers in crisp-blue jackets—Lieutenant-major Taylor raised a long-gleaming saber, his mouth flying open like a stallion screaming—Major Nicholson pumped a rifle, bellowing. Had they heard of Donaldson? They whooped as the governor rode by, and I waited, bolstering my courage, and Taylor swept me down with a single glance, and Nicholson nodded wildly, and they laughed at Young Andrew who had changed his mind and rode now only three rows behind the militia's commander-in-chief.

I stared ahead, cool and disciplined on the outside, edgy on the inside, our orders to keep on our march.

The Nez Perce and Nicholson's battalion fell in behind us, and we encamped that evening at the old Whitman station, and I picketed my gray mare in a lush-looking site of rye grass, and Nicholson and Taylor came down into the wallow, Nicholson sneering, chewing his mustache, Taylor snapping glances all around, acting vindicated in an angry way.

"Know what you found?" asked Nicholson.

I stared at him blankly.

"I told you long ago, didn't I? The Cayuse dumped Narcissa Whitman here. It's the irrigation ditch the Whitmans dug."

I glared at him as if he had never said anything of the sort, and he and Taylor stepped nearer, smelling of whiskey like everyone else that summer. They spread and planted their feet, and Nicholson pulled out a tanned Indian scrotum and worked his pipe inside for tobacco. "The Cayuse did more than kill and cut and burn that day. They took a girl newly blooming, not fourteen yet." Nicholson dropped the scrotum back inside his shirt, struck a match against a pistol-butt, fired the pipe, jabbed it at a grove of locust. "They had her over there, the blood of her mother and father still on their knives. They took the wife of an emigrant, his blood still on their hands. They took another and told her they would cut up her mother and father if she did not submit. Only the Lord knows how many they took."

"I hear you've been confessing," said Taylor. "Spreading stories."

"No sir," I said.

"I am not doomed." Taylor gunned me a vicious look. "I don't give a god damn what you say, but if you accuse me again to anyone, I will silence your blabber for good."

"Yes sir," I said, and I chased Lalooh from my mind, beat her away with a stick, for I suspected the two knew everything I had told the governor, and they understood Lalooh could speak in English about Dry Creek.

Most of the Nez Perce headed home, taking a pack train east, and Pretty Jim and the governor led us south along an old Indian trail, and we climbed into the Blue Mountains at night, hiding our dust, all our companies ready for action, Nicholson's battalion making us nearly two hundred sixty strong. We encamped amid fir, the wind moaning coolly, and we rested our animals a day and then descended into the smell of sulfur and soda springs, and we halted on a knoll and saw a dust cloud winding several miles down along the Grande Ronde.

"The treaty designates that stretch partly to Old Joseph of the Nez Perce, partly to the Cayuse and Wallawalla," said the governor.

"They are not Nez Perce," said Pretty Jim.

Two Cayuse warriors, Panther and Long Elk, rode halfway up the knoll and signed to us. *We have no chiefs here to talk. We wish for translators.*

Dominique and I rode down with Jim and the governor, and we halted in scattered pine, leaving our first column of troops close behind.

Long Elk waved for Jim to parley—braves were already fanning out in the river-bottoms below us—squaws were scurrying, carrying bundles—horses were sputtering, neighing—lodge poles were clattering down.

Jim and the governor rode forth, a U.S. Army bandolier hanging down Jim's painted chest, U.S. medals on the belt-strap, the strap's pockets stuffed with cartridges for his new Sharp's rifle.

"Look at his gifts!" cried a Cayuse.

"Shoot him!" cried another.

Jim wheeled on his horse, and the governor followed, galloping past me, yelling uphill, "Form lines! Charge!"

The bugles sounded. The horses thundered down, and the braves fell back into brush, separating, and Dominique went right, veering with the governor, another detachment went left, and I descended straight with Nicholson, charging the middle, and a squaw ran toward the river, her shoulder slumping, and Taylor lifted a rifle, and he shot, and the squaw fell, and troops galloped across her, others pressing behind me, branches whipping and cracking, voices screaming, quirts snapping, guns firing and flashing. And I was swept past her, and she looked too old, too easily crushed to be Lalooh, but I got only a glimpse, galloping, and then another Cayuse lay in the cinder-dirt, a shriveled face, a throat riddled with balls, and then another, an old man face down, and the brush opened to a road, and packs were strewn everywhere, and horses ran half-loaded, spilling Indian gear, and a spear rose behind a saddle, and *Bang!* Another squaw fell, and rifles clapped, and braves fell behind rocks, and then we slowed, clustering in pines again, muskets popping across a ford, arrows whizzing, Indians fighting from inside a thick shield of alder.

"They think they can feign a retreat and ambush us," said the governor.

Our marksmen knelt, fired across the water, and the governor rode back and forth behind them, leaning forward on a white stallion, his face slick and red and sweaty, leaf-bits in his beard, eyes shining gigantically, reins in one hand, Sharp's rifle smoking in the other. "No prisoners! No mercy! Do not the fear the devil who would take your flesh!"

"Eaton! Dominique!" Taylor came on foot, holding a squaw squirming against his waist, and he shoved her toward me, yanking a braid, and her head snapped up, her nose and mouth bloody, her cheeks arched high like Lalooh's, her stare young and hateful, and I barked down at her, translating Taylor's questions.

"Who are your chiefs?"

"Who are yours?" she said. "Killers, volunteers, not regulars!"

Taylor yanked a braid farther, his smirk long and lanky like his body, his eyes tall and bulging, bugging out rapturously.

I barked his next question, "How many warriors?"

"Ten!" cried the squaw. "Maybe twelve! We are just old men and women here for the springs, just women digging roots!"

"Ten?" Taylor flung her, and men dragged her behind a tree, pushing her to her knees, and their guns fired, and I remained on my horse, watching her legs go limp, the men fall upon her with knives, and then I looked about, hoping for Dominique, and a ball crashed through a bough above me, and I got off, was passed a shovel, and I dug ground pits until Nicholson hallooed, galloping aside the governor and Pretty Jim.

The three busted down the bank, firing revolvers, and I followed, my gray slipping on bedrock, lunging, recovering, but others fell, splashing tremendous sprays, and Nicholson led, whipping his horse across the ford, and *Pop!* A red wad of hair flew behind him, and he shook visibly, kept firing, kept smashing through brush, and troops closed behind him, gaining the bank too, and I spread out with them, chasing Indians fleeing on ponies. And braves turned in timber, firing muskets and bows, making a stand, and Taylor whooped, lifting his saber, and our company converged, rode directly at the threat, and the braves dispersed again, and squaws and children ran in the far side the river, stumbling, grabbing for one another, and we slowed to a trot, and Taylor and others lifted rifles deliberately, and then the river swung our way, and an Indian boy dove, and his mother knelt in rapids, clasping her hands, begging, and other squaws tore off clothes, showing their sex, and an order came from the bend behind them, the governor's marksmen hidden in more alder. "Fire!" Shots came from both banks, clouds of lead, and squaws and children flew, thrashing, wailing, and the mother still knelt, bleeding, weeping, bodies sweeping past her, and the next round came, and then every Indian there was down, and I was up in my saddle, waving my six-shooter, shrieking myself hoarse with my company, and we sped on, gaining a buffalo robe lying on our bank, and I drew rein, and Taylor aimed suddenly beside me, firing with others, and the robe flew into the water, revealing three boys below, bunched against a log-sweep, eyes wide and horrified—then peppered with bullets.

"Lodges!" Taylor cried, and my company rode hollering and shooting on, balls and bullets thumping against the tules, pinging against poles, and some men dismounted, pulled open door-flaps, fired inside, and others pulled the lodges apart.

Northcroft from Steilacoom and Farveaux from White River pulled a squaw along the ground, each dragging an arm, and they stopped before Taylor, and he dismounted, and she rolled toward him, lifting a hand, a white cloth. "No mercy!" yelled Taylor. "No prisoners!" He swung his sword, knocked her body flat, her arm crooked, an artery spurting. She rolled grabbing it, and a musket popped, spraying a legging, and she turned, lifting the other arm, and Taylor swung again, slicing and smashing her good shoulder, and someone else shot, hitting her skull, and Taylor mounted again. He hitched himself high, screaming toward another lodge, and I spurred my gray mare round and round it, my six-shooter in my hand, the hammer cocked, and no one came out, and I was about to shoot, empty my chambers into tules. I would look the part again, I thought. I would disarm myself, take a ball, take an arrow, but Taylor yelled again, staring down at sacks of beans, flour, coffee, sugar, digging sticks, boxes of army beef, bags of roots. "Seize them!" He turned to me again. "Eaton!" He pointed at an old brave shouting from steam-clouds on a ledge behind a lodge, wearing nothing but ear pendants, screaming denouncements too fast to comprehend, and *Bang!* The brave flew backward into a bubbling pool, and the water streamed bloodily down the lip of the white-crusted rock. "What did he say?" cried Taylor.

I could not speak. I was sure Taylor would die for his wickedness. I thought Nicholson had already fallen.

"You lie to me, it's treason!" said Taylor.

"I did not hear!"

He raised his revolver. I raised mine.

Shots clapped way beyond the village, and Taylor glanced begrudgingly, and he lowered his gun, and I lowered mine.

We rode toward the shots and came to a prairie—to a white soldier laid out in tall-wet grass, his groin hit and bleeding heavily, a mortal wound—to another, a bullet wound in the nose—another with a cheek dangling down against his neck—another all black from wrestling in mud, a piece of his head resting on his chest, chopped by a hatchet.

And Dominique stood beyond a bend in the river, ramming his rifle down, driving its bayonet again and again into an old Cayuse who had laid behind the bank and had picked off volunteers as they had emerged into the clearing.

Dominique's hat fell, his hair flopped, his shoulders heaved, and he grunted like a beast, gasping, not realizing, and *Bang!* The governor rose way out in the blue blooms of the camas lilies, his rifle smoking again, and he crouched, loading, and Nicholson stood ably from behind a spruce stump and firmly shouldered his Sharp's. He shot, and another report came from the governor, and an Indian flew and fell crookedly, looking withered and hunchbacked, and he thrashed in camas stems, and then the lilies went still.

The whole prairie went still, the entire valley—no noises but the chuff and slosh of Dominique's bayonet, and Taylor muttering tersely to troops, bending over our mangled men, telling others to fix up litters and bandages.

And then flames crackled and roared—tules and lodge-poles—and I turned as if ordered. I rode as if on a mission, skirting and jumping over bronze bodies, counting them as if directed by God, but not stopping. Old men, old women. Skinless children. Mutilations unspeakable. The squaw with butchered arms, her privates stretched over a pommel, a trampled papoose, a busted cradleboard, mashed camas mush, the baby's victuals.

I crossed the ford and rode through trampled brush powdered with soil-grit, passing one corpse looking like Panther's, another like Long Elk's, the innards where each had been cut glistening moistly in the sun through the battle dust.

And I was not sure, for many dead braves might lay hidden, but I thought the squaw killed in the pines at the ford had spoken truly—perhaps the Cayuse had only a dozen young warriors in camp, for we had destroyed the village only a couple hours after we had discovered it.

I approached the knoll, and the squaw with the slumping shoulder lay dead, her body the same rusty-red color as the soil-grit, the dirt a kind of a blessing, for it darkened places where she had been broken open. A head strap lay on the ground—Lalooh's? Both shoulders were slumped, were battered now. The back of her hair was crushed and matted and told me nothing, but I dismounted, feeling a cold pit of certainty, and I knelt and turned her and emptied my canteen, rinsing bone-splinters, blood, brain-ooze from her face.

A horse snorted above me. "See how you are wrong?" Nicholson looked down from his saddle, a hole and powder burns in his beard, and I reached and found my holster empty, my revolver dropped somewhere.

Nicholson watched my fingers clutch, smiling, and he reached beneath his beard, pulling a ball from where it had stuck in his jacket. "You thought I would be punished, and the Cayuse would not. But the Ruler of the Universe—He who takes vengeance on the guilty—did not design it so, and thus you have prisoners waiting, their lies to decipher."

He nodded me back to the river, and I grabbed my gray's reins, indicating her spent condition, and I walked slowly as if pushing against an onrushing nightmare, and I entered a half-circle of men standing before a Cayuse boy tied to a tree, a bruise and gash closing one of his eyes, a bandage tied to the side of his head, an ear badly wounded. Pretty Jim knelt before him, asking questions, and the boy spat, and Jim rose, lifting a quirt, and I barked, and he and Taylor and Nicholson turned, and I stood testing their stares, raging, and then I felt the river tinkling behind me, the sound racing coldly up my spine, gurgling into everyone's silence, and the governor spoke only several trees away, dictating to Dominique.

"*My Honorable Major Edward Wells—The volunteer force under the command of Major Benjamin Nicholson and myself have struck the hostile Indians a severe blow in the Grande Ronde, where they had collected to the number of four hundred warriors—at the very spot where Kamiakin launched his federation. We engaged hostiles in a running fight for fifteen miles and killed at least sixty. We captured at least three hundred horses, one hundred fifty packs of supplies and considerable ammunition. We will auction the animals in particular to defray the cost of the entire expedition.*

"*The war between the Cascades and Rockies is clearly over, clearly won. The army claims to have the hostiles in hand north of the Columbia, and the Washington Militia has defeated the last stronghold south of it.*

"*Pretty Jim tells me some Nez Perce have grown restless, mainly due to the conciliations the army has dealt to hostile chiefs and tribes. But after I announce our victory in Olympia, I will proceed to the Walla Walla council grounds again in September with the object of the pacification of all tribes.*

"*All innocent chiefs and tribes must attend and turn in Kamiakin, Owhi and all others who started the war. I suggest you at once send a force including all your mounted men, say three companies, to occupy and secure Walla Walla Valley until then.*"

We encamped amid the pines and along an arch of the river, keeping guard all night, and at dawn I started directly to the squaw again, but I stopped at the sight of Dominique's head on a ledge across the river, his eyes closed as if in eternal sleep, his mouth wrinkled as if from whatever brutality he had suffered. I nearly shouted an alarm. I gazed all about. I started across the river, and his eyes popped open, and I approached and nearly shuddered anew—Dominique was seeking relief in a jade-colored mineral bath, not beheaded as I feared, but discolored from yesterday's bruises.

"I am sorry, Andrew," he said, "there were no Yakama here, only Cayuse and a few Wallawalla and Umatilla. You need not worry."

Part of a load lifted from me, for if I reasoned with myself, I knew I had not seen any Yakama either.

"What about four hundred warriors?"

"A few fierce old bastards were enough, were they not?"

I swallowed my objection—all Americans shot at the prairie had died.

"Come," he said, "get in."

I got in, wanting to feel warm, clean—and to keep close to Dominique, and he knew why, of course.

"Nicholson and Taylor think you sympathize too much. They think you will never forget Dry Creek."

"Nicholson will never forget Narcissa Whitman, will he?"

"And nor will I, my friend. When the Cayuse killed her, they made all of this their fate—as the Whitmans made it theirs, and the governor makes it his, and you and I make it ours. You see, when the Whitmans arrived in 'thirty-six, Narcissa was a fair-skinned angel where none had ever existed before. When I first saw her, I was bringing the mission a heating stove and window sashes, and she was shoveling clamshells on a fire, making whitewash in a smoke that smelled as rank as bloated whales. Yet Narcissa looked immaculate, hailing my wagon—her long-golden hair tied exquisitely with a broach—her face smooth, radiant, delicately lipped—her eyes two freshets in a desert, breath-catching blue—sure of everything they took in, apt to turn instantly gray and moody at anything that displeased her measure.

"Narcissa was slender and well-formed, not bandy-legged and pug-faced and brown. Any man could see the strength in her, and when you heard her sing, you heard a voice from heaven—squaws brought their children from all directions, not understanding a word, but enchanted by the refinement of her tones." Dominique reached for his shirt behind him, lowered it into the pool, wrung out yesterday's blood. "Narcissa remained upright, no matter the challenge. She never relinquished her higher calling, and she always abided her husband, no matter the task the reverend tackled, or the means he insisted upon. He crossed the virgin continent, plowed the virgin sod, planted and harvested it, built and preached upon it. He did not like to stop his work and talk with the Cayuse, no! They asked him why he broke the ground where camas and celery already grew, and he whipped his oxen and pushed his plow onward. They asked him if he did not think the winter rain would wash away his house, and he kept making adobes. They asked him if it was not wrong to steal their timber, and he turned his wagon to the hills for another load. They told him he brought too many emigrants, and he showed them the Protestant Ladder and translated Bible stories and told them he would bring shiploads of American sailors to punish them."

Can you stop the whites from coming? Can you stop the rivers? The wind? Cannons will come here—and here—and here—and here.

"The Whitmans were destined to die, I think," said Dominique. "Marcus saw the Indians as a lost race, and Narcissa wanted them out of her house away from her chinaware, and they knew it. The Whitmans told the Cayuse they built a mission to bring God to Indians, but emigrants came instead. A month before they were murdered, a brave came to my post and recited the names of all the Cayuse the reverend had killed since he had arrived. He said the Indians got a fever and rash, they shat blood and snot, and then they died. I told him they had the measles, and he said Marcus had brought poison in a bottle from Boston and had given it to Cayuse, so he could save the souls of whites, not Indians."

"Narcisse?" I said. "Narcissa?"

"Yes, but I gave him the name for the sheer beauty—before I understood the rest."

Dominique wrung the blood from his drawers and socks.

"Have you talked with the governor?" I asked. "About his council?"

"No, but we're going west, and he's sending you north to take a dispatch to Wells."

"Alone?"

"Pretty Jim will escort you to Mill Creek and then turn east with another dispatch to Lawyer and Looking Glass."

"The governor, Taylor and Nicholson want me dead."

"Not the governor. He has seen and heard how you avoid danger on a horse. He would not send you if he were not sure you would get through."

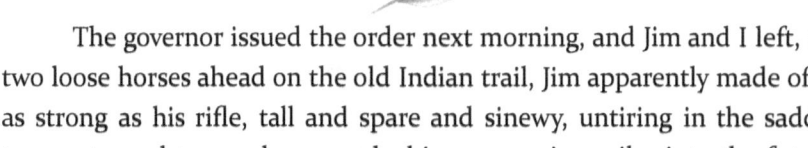

The governor issued the order next morning, and Jim and I left, driving two loose horses ahead on the old Indian trail, Jim apparently made of a steel as strong as his rifle, tall and spare and sinewy, untiring in the saddle, his tongue turned to wood, no words, his eyes seeing miles into the future. We raced through our old fir camp, and he looked up, and a brave gazed down from a pony on an outcrop, unflinching, bare-chested and bare-legged, Cayuse-looking, and when the timber opened, we saw dust in trees behind us, heard hooves pounding, Cayuse shrieking, "Kill the white! Kill the traitor!"

The hooves and war-whoops swooped down after us, and Jim descended the trail, leaping brush and downfalls and creek-crossings, and then his horse's tail flounced, turning, and I jerked my gray after it, and boulders met us withers-high, and my gray leaped, plunged into a feeder stream, buckled withers-deep, and she lunged out through devil's club, the thorns slashing, cutting, and the brush gave way to a soft-needled game trail, and we ascended, rounding a ridge, reaching a rock slide, and Jim followed it straight up and then waited on a mountain-top, saddling his second Appaloosa, watching thirty Cayuse hedging on their ponies in a creek-clearing a half-world below.

Jim tossed dried camas unsmiling into his mouth, plunder from the Grande Ronde, the same kind of roots Lalooh had brought me in her baskets. He walked around the horses, daubing pine pitch on their cuts, and then we rode into granddaddy trees as dark, cold and brooding as his mood, and we climbed into shafts of sunlight nearly blinding, crossing divides along the crusty edges of snowfields. We descended a washed-out road, passing trees with deep rings around trunks, scars from early emigrants who had lowered wagons by ropes, and then we wound down gulches to immense-steep slopes of open grass, suspicious stands of isolated trees, and the air grew hot again, the sun low, the shadows long.

Gunfire popped beyond the next hill, and Jim and I dismounted, crept to its crest and lay watching while warriors—Cayuse and Nez Perce—galloped on a plain below, descending through the quick-coming twilight into a shrubby ditch, lowering muskets and then raising them again as they rode out. Squaws were kneeling darkly in the shrubs, reloading and passing up the guns, and the braves fanned out toward the Walla Walla River, moving toward a circle of un-mounted mules and horses, the animals braying and screaming, rearing and tugging against lines tied to packs left on the ground—a white supply train, no packers anywhere.

"Do you recognize any of the Nez Perce?" I whispered. "Anyone from Lawyer's band?"

"Lawyer will be sorry for the Cayuse," said Jim. "But our band will never attack the whites."

And then the moon rose full, flooding the tops of cottonwoods down beside the river, and braves dismounted, diving into the dark below the trees, whooping as they pilfered, and a string of packers ran from the far side of the trees, fuzzy forms on foot, fleeing into more cottonwoods.

And squaws emerged suddenly from a ditch directly below us, just out of rifle range, and Lalooh led a piebald, and a brave met her, lifting and shaking new flannel shirts, the plumes of his war cap the longest I had ever seen, swiping the grass. Skistymay. And Nammakin strutted up in his wolf-eared cap, patting the piebald, waving shirts too, and Lalooh hoisted a pack to his work horse, her shoulder working rhythmically, looking healed, and I looked toward Pretty Jim, wondering now if he recognized her, and the moonlight showed flattened grass beside me, spikes of seed-heads, shadows of my horses behind me, but not Jim. He had crept off, and I was not surprised.

Forty or fifty mounted warriors passed beneath me, then horses and mules strapped and packed, then squaws bunched too tightly to distinguish, then a rear guard of braves. Sinkiuse. Yakama. Nez Perce. Cayuse. All working in accord.

The Indians trotted around a slope, disappearing, and I went to my gray, pulled the time ball from a pack, stuffed it in my shirt, and I took my horses down to the party's tracks, and I felt queasy, sick with her, my fingers trembling on my reins, my soul still tasting hope, the sharp surge of seeing her, and then I rode up to the next crest and studied the hills and the silver thread below, the river.

No Lalooh.

No campfires.

No whiskey whoops.

No other camp sounds.

A flame billowed suddenly across the valley, a tall-dead pine burning on a butte, a signal fire. Another blazed east, another farther north, all too far to be Lalooh's party, each seeming to say the governor had no need to go to Olympia to announce his victory at Grande Ronde. The word was already out.

Pom-poms drummed distantly north, and I gathered courage and yelled east, "La-looh!" My voice rose hoarsely, weakly. I heard no reply. I drew more breath and bellowed, standing in stirrups, "LA-LOOH!"

A white man yelled from behind me, "Hal-lo!"

"LA-LOOH!" I yelled again. *"ITITA'MAT!"*

"Here!" yelled the white. "Hal-lo! Ambushed! Help!"

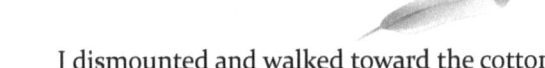

I dismounted and walked toward the cottonwoods back by the river, and the man waved his hat above the grass, hobbling on a leg that had been kicked by a panicked mule, the moon lighting up his narrow-beak nose, cheeks fleshy from years of drink, white spots on his neck scarf—Polka Dot Leggett—a packer known to work teams up the Columbia and Okanogan to the customs house and beyond.

"Did you kill any?" he asked, eyeing the rifle in my saddle holster.

"No," I said. "I have to keep on. I have an express for Major Wells."

"Tell Wells to kill 'em all, every last one. Tell him we fought hundreds a' hostiles all afternoon, and I didn't lose a single man, and I seen some hostiles to name—the Sinkiuse chief and the Yakama warrior whose squaw talks for them—Sparkling Water. They got seven thousand dollars worth—all my gold dust! Red-flannel shirts! Boots! Doctor Stevens' Remedy! A new anvil! A bellows!" He glared ruefully east. "You ride your bay to Wells, and I'll give you fifty dollars for your gray. I'll write you a note for dust."

"I can't take a note."

"The hell you can't!"

At least a dozen pairs of eyes peered from the cottonwood-edge, shining as fearfully as those of the boys beneath the robe on the Grande Ronde. "Kanakas," said Leggett. "Sandwich Islanders. They don't speak English, but I couldn't hire anyone else to help pack 'tween here and Astoria. Every white man is doing what you're doing—drawing pay, hunting hostiles."

"The governor just killed seventy or eighty on the Grande Ronde, mostly squaws and kids and old Cayuse," I said.

Leggett considered the news, looking around at the signal fires. "I could a' kept my team if the Kanakas could a' understood me," he said. "I had 'em take the packs off my stock and then lay down and shoot from behind 'em. But it got dark, and we run out of ammo, and I called a retreat. You stay here tonight and go to Wells tomorrow. We got nothing to eat, nothing to drink. You go tonight, they'll kill you anyhow."

I shook my head no, heading to the Kanakas, and Leggett huffed loudly, hobbling hard, and the more he talked and looked at my canteens, the more my gray balled her yellow eyes, shying from him, and the farther I pulled my horses from the cottonwoods.

Two Kanakas stepped fully from the trees, then three, then more. Each gestured for water.

"They won't go down to the river," said Leggett. "They think the Indians are waiting."

I gave Leggett my canteens and all the Grande Ronde salmon I had packed, and he went to his Kanakas, and I pulled a pair of hobbles from my saddle, and I kept my distance, posting both horses, and I listened again, for I knew I had not waited long enough after I had called Lalooh's name, and I thought some power in her could watch me from the moon, all of us if she wished.

Leggett returned, the empty canteens knocking carelessly, and then he clattered down to the river and clattered back, the canteens still empty. "You hear it?" he whispered. I stared toward the nearest pom-poms. "No, not that-a-way. Listen across the river." Some kind of organ approached, a voice rose through the drums. "A squeezebox," said Leggett, and he spotted my saddle on the ground, dropped the canteens, pulled my rifle from the saddle holster, checked the chamber. "Kamiakin's priest. Funny how he shows up after all the shooting's done—like he never tells the Indians nothing."

Father Sidalia sang in his deepest-finest tones, stretching every sacred sound. "*A-ve Mar-i-a gra-tia ple-na, Mar-i-a grat-i-a ple-na!*"

Leggett hobbled hastily downhill again, and I followed, drawing my pistol, but the accordion flexed plainly across the water, its ivory keys flooded by moonbeams. Sidalia appeared to be alone. He cantered nearly into the rifle's range, his teeth and dimples stretching, gleaming, his bare feet milky and pale beneath the darkness of his gown—his music was announcing his presence, so any savage in the night would know and spare him.

"*A-ve a-ve dom-i-nus! Dom-i-nus te-cum! In mul-i-er-i-bus!*" He sang while looking for a ford. "*Et ben-e-dic-tus! Et be-ne-dic-tus!*" The horse shuffled to a beaten bank, and then its hooves picked their way through water, and Sidalia quieted, raising his chin toward the cottonwoods—the Kanakas thudded along the bank, and the first knelt, then the others, and they crossed themselves.

"*Ventris tui Jsus,*" sang the lead Kanaka.

"*Ave Maria, Ave Maria,*" sang the others. "*Sancta Maria.*"

Leggett's eyes shone a long, disappointed look at me. "The Pope wants the whole world, nothing less," he muttered, and he thrust the rifle against my chest, and Sidalia caught the motion, hearing me clasp the barrel, and I cried his name.

"Eaton!" he cried.

"Are you alone, Father?"

"No, look ye!" Sidalia pointed behind us. "None of us are alone! She has placed His cross upon the moon!" The Kanakas swung their heads, exclaiming in their own tongue, and I saw only gray patches upon the moon, bluish wisps. "She has brought us together at this crossing—you and I and these pilgrims here! This country swarms with rumors, and Major Wells sent me to find the truth!"

Sidalia dismounted on the south bank, speaking Polynesian, and the Kanakas answered, and he walked among them, touching their heads, giving them blessings, and they kissed his gown and feet, fingering the squeezebox, smiling wondrously at the moon.

Leggett howled as we approached, "They're under my employ, Father! What are you telling them? We've just been attacked by hundreds a' your Indians!"

"Then be quiet, so they don't attack you again," said Sidalia.

"You admit they're yours?"

"No, Wells sent me to look for them. He's making lines for a new fort, and he wants the Indians to know the army will protect them as well as whites. General Wool has issued a new order. The interior is closed to any new settlement."

"Wool ought to be hanged!" shouted Leggett. "Wells ought to be hanged! You should be wrung up a tree and nailed!"

The Kanakas swung their gazes from voice to voice, remaining on their knees, and Sidalia motioned them up and turned to Leggett. "Look ye at the moon, poor man!"

"They ain't no cross!" said Leggett.

There were wavy-dark lines perhaps, shadowy shapes amid gray patches, and Leggett quickened his hobbling, clenching his fists, and Sidalia slung the squeezebox against his hip, glaring at me to keep myself contained, his crucifix beaming white. "I told them the Immaculate Heart protects them, and they must stay with the captain of the mule train," said Sidalia. "You must go at sunrise to Wells and march with a white flag and cross, and Mary will continue to protect all of you. Her miracle is now the only way, just as He has always been. The Indians think a village of Cayuse has been massacred by the governor. Wells got word, and I told him I would go immediately to any band I could find."

"You so cozy with the Indians, you tell 'em to bring back what they stole."

"It doesn't sound like they're in any such mood. Who attacked you, Mister Leggett, Kamiakin?"

Leggett swung his fist, and Sidalia slumped at the stomach, gasping, and then his chin reeled, crunching from an uppercut, and some of the Kanakas shoved Leggett uphill, knocking my grip from his shoulder, their hands all over him, and others knelt around Sidalia as he lay upon the ground, wiping his mouth.

I barely knew I had grabbed Leggett—he had waved himself free, barking at his charges, and now he spat my way, stepping above Sidalia again, glaring down silently, his hat knocked off, his temples pulsing, pom-poms pounding louder, nearer the river.

Another signal fire raced like a fuse up a tree, flaming from a nearer butte, and I heard my voice before I knew I spoke. "There has been a massacre, Father Sidalia. I am coming from it. I took part in it. I must go with you."

We left Leggett and his Kanakas in the cottonwoods and followed the Indians' retreat trail across the bunchgrass hills, the moon climbing ever-higher, the lines on its face looking sketchier, wavering, yet Sidalia watched them fervently, still singing boldly, playing his squeezebox.

Glass shards twinkled beside hoof-prints—the jars of Doctor Stevens' Tonic smashed. The trail veered toward the river again, and a whiskey stench rose—barrels hacked to pieces by the river—a sign of the war party's resolve—the prospect of drunken braves poured away into the thirsty earth.

Little-dark mounds floated strangely uphill from the bank, and warriors circled us, moving deliberately on foot. Many of them wore red-flannel shirts and shreds of polka dot bandanas dangling beside war charms, and they raised guns and bows, and Sidalia sang of Mary, slipping in Salish words he had learned during his banishment to Sinkiuse and Spokane country. He looked gravely down at warriors, then up at the moon, and a knife whistled through the dark, and the squeezebox thumped, belched, wheezed. The blade's handle stuck out the bellows, and I held up a white rag, yelling in Yakama, "We come in peace! We have a message from Major Wells!"

Sidalia flew from his horse, seized by braves, and I yelled his name, mine, and gun barrels approached, and I remembered to show no quarter, keep my voice steady, reveal no sentiment for my companion. "We wish to parley with your chiefs," I said. "To speak through Lalooh."

Nammakin grinned up suddenly, standing beside my gray, and he yanked me off, and another brave took my horse, another my rifle, another my pistol, and I was shoved against Sidalia, who stood restrained while a brave worked the squeezebox beside him, laughing as it sputtered.

My head snapped backward—Nammakin fisted my hair, whooshed a blade above my nape, cut a tuft, spun me, fisted my shirt, tore it. The beaded hemp fell. He knelt and then rose, pulling the time ball from the bag. "Crooked Hair," he growled. "Our Words Against Us. Dry Creek Boy."

"I am waiting," I said, standing square-shouldered, my hands compliant at my hips. "If you do not kill me, I am ashamed."

"We will not kill you as cowards killed Peopeomoxmox," he said. "Not yet."

Sidalia heard his English and cried out, "See the moon! The One who loves you most has placed His cross upon it! He weeps for the dead at Grande Ronde! For the governor and his militia!"

The white rag was torn from my hand, stuffed into Sidalia's mouth, and we were pushed forward, and mounted braves galloped ahead as we walked parallel to the Walla Walla, Nammakin leading, other braves clucking and yipping beside us, still flourishing weapons. We ascended a creek and entered the Indians' camp, and Sidalia hummed prayers through his gag, looking only at the moon, blue-gray shadows rippling down through the center now, cutting a figure dissolving behind the gray patches one moment, darkening the next, shifting, writhing. We entered a lodge, and Quiltenenock and Skistymay sat stern-faced behind the fire, their chests and faces painted a bloodthirsty blue, barbaric circles painted red and yellow around their eyes. A brave untied Sidalia's mouth-rag, and then Lalooh padded soundlessly inside and bent gracefully before Quiltenenock and Nammakin. She placed a large Yakama medicine bag beside a Sinkiuse bag, her beaded buckskin tucking lithely to her body, her hair as wet-gleaming as it had been on her dawn-log at the treaty council, as if she had been scalp-dancing again and had readied herself in a hurry to help attend white prisoners. She rose from the bags, and her gaze remained as elusive as at Camp Naches, and our danger merely sharpened my sorrow, and Sidalia knew, and he glanced at me warily.

Quiltenenock unwrapped the Sinkiuse bag, lifted a long-stemmed pipe, packed it. He lifted a coal with a wooden tongue and lit the tobacco. The Sinkiuse pipe went around twice, and then Nammakin opened the Yakama bag, and the Yakama pipe went around twice, and Sidalia gently clasped his rosary. "The Immaculate Heart protects us in our anguish—all of us." He clasped his crucifix. "She has placed the cross of Jesus Christ upon the moon, and the Savior looks down upon us tonight and spreads His love." Sidalia spoke a prayer in Sinkiuse, and Quiltenenock gazed blankly away, and then Sidalia prayed in Yakama, looking at Lalooh, and she said nothing.

Nammakin stood reaching into a small flour sack I had hidden in the bottom of a saddlebag before I had left the Grande Ronde. He pulled out the governor's letter and handed it to Quiltenenock, showing no knowledge of its contents, for he spoke but did not read English.

Quiltenenock broke the seal eagerly and handed the letter to Lalooh, and her beautiful copper gaze roamed its contents, and then she spoke the letter in Sinkiuse and Yakama, and Quiltenenock sat clawing his chest, rubbing the anger swelling there. "Bloody Beard and Rotten Wind have not won the war," he said. "They killed old men and women, and you carry their lies."

"Yes," grunted Lalooh. "He stole the *itita'mat*."

"Let us kill the black robe in payment for Almcotty," said Nammakin.

"Let us kill Bloody Beard for Long Elk and Rotten Wind for Panther," said Skistymay.

"Let us kill Trader Purcell for Weshanaberts," said Nammakin, "and Dry Creek Boy for his lies and stealing the *itita'mat*."

"No, Andrew did not steal the *itita'mat*," said Sidalia. "Trader Purcell found it left behind at Camp Naches, and Andrew has broken the law of Rotten Wind to return it. Andrew might have carried Rotten Wind's paper to Major Wells by now. But he came to Quiltenenock first, and Rotten Wind would hang him if he knew. The good medicine guides Andrew, not the bad. I beseech you! Let us go look at the moon!"

Quiltenenock spoke rapidly, and Lalooh translated, "Your holy son does not make the marks on the moon. The Sinkiuse dreamt a moon like this years ago, and then we went with the Yakama across the mountains, and buffalo came from every direction."

"The devil speaks in you, the old superstitions," said Sidalia. "The Son of God weeps when you leave your gardens and hunt His beasts. He has heard the prayers of Indians who plant the land, and He has blessed them with His bounty."

Skistymay spoke vehemently, and Lalooh translated, "The black robe also tells the lies of his people. We must kill every spirit doctor of the whites."

"The black robe has not come to hurt you," I said. "He has defied the governor just as I have. He has come to tell you that General Wool has closed your land to white settlement. But sometimes the black robe has his own devil inside him, and he does not know how to speak about beasts and farming.

"It is true, I came to return the *itita'mat*, and if Rotten Wind knew, he would hang me. But hear me, my friends! I deserve to be hanged by Lalooh and Nammakin, not by the governor. I am Andrew Eaton, son of Samuel and Alicia Eaton of Beaufort, Illinois..." I recited the words I had rehearsed so many times to myself, and then I went on. "I have sinned both my people and yours. I was afraid to raise a hand three days ago when Rotten Wind and Bloody Beard killed so many Cayuse. And I was even more afraid when I looked upon a squaw with brains oozing from her head, for I thought she was Lalooh. But I see Lalooh here, and I no longer fear for myself. You can take me, and I will make a blood payment to the relatives at Dry Creek and the Grande Ronde. I will make a horse or gold payment, or you may whip, deface or kill me. I am waiting."

Lalooh spoke my words to Quiltenenock, her head still stiffly turned, her eyelashes flicking spitefully, and Sidalia rasped beside me, his breath ticking with a kind of a subdued panting, his gaze loathing me, and Quiltenenock and Skistymay gradually widened their eyes, listening to Lalooh, drawing my stare into theirs, and Nammakin seemed not to breathe at all, feeling contempt to the depth of his bones.

Quiltenenock looked at Lalooh, and she spoke the letter to him again, and he motioned for her to return it to the flour sack.

"He is a coward," she said. "He does not know how to live."

Quiltenenock nodded in agreement and spoke to her again, and she translated in a seething hush, peering only at Sidalia. "Both of you will sleep here in this lodge tonight. Nammakin, Skistymay and others will escort you at dawn, and you will go straight to the major. The black robe need not visit other bands, for all the Indians already know about Grande Ronde and the major's new fort. You will tell Wells we have spared the black robe and Dry Creek Boy, and we will attend the new council, so Rotten Wind can turn his lies into truth. Quiltenenock will meet with the governor, and they will settle our lines."

She handed Sidalia the flour sack and rose and padded out as the priest passed it to me.

"Four hundred warriors!" grunted Quiltenenock, the first and only English I ever heard him speak. He muttered unintelligibly to Nammakin and Skistymay and then stared at the lodge-fire as if he were already scheming, hoping to win the return of the Sinkiuse land and fishing grounds.

Nammakin and Skistymay allowed Sidalia his dawn prayers, and afterward we rode in a string of warriors, turning from the Walla Walla, winding in and out of gulch after gulch. We leapt a little-rocky run, Nammakin shrieked, and I looked, and there was the defile, a glimpse of the narrow-green bottoms, walls of chalky-gray columns above Dry Creek, and braves galloped beside me, snarling, shouting insolently in Salish. They shook spears and muskets and yelled in Chinook from both sides. *"Diáub'!" Devil! "Skoo'kum!" Demon!*

But Skistymay shouted in Sinkiuse, leading the party, hurrying, and the braves fell away, and we muscled our mounts up and around towering slopes of grass all morning, and finally cannons boomed nearby, and we saw a flash like a mirror atop a butte.

The Indians wheeled, and Sidalia and I ascended freely to the flash, a team of sappers sighting a sextant at a dish of mercury. The sappers had not seen the Indians, but when they saw Sidalia, they snapped to attention. They saluted him dutifully, and he responded in kind, and we proceeded across the summit alone and then gazed upon the broad-open valley below—Mill Creek meeting the Walla Walla, the tents of four companies pitched just above the old mission site, Dragoons drilling with artillery teams, howitzers firing blanks—a response to last night's drums—Wells' posturing.

Sidalia and I had not spoken since the parley, and I looked at him squarely, and he wrenched his countenance bitterly. "I lament all the red souls you have lost," he said. "I grieve for yours, Eaton."

He galloped headlong downhill, and I followed him to the major's tent and waited as he went in and conferred with Wells, and then Sidalia came out brusquely, ignoring me with a coolness that rivaled Lalooh's.

Wells watched from behind the door flaps, and I saluted and entered, and he grasped my hand heartily, embraced me, gave me brandy, insisted I dine on sirloin while he sat sweating, pondering the governor's letter upon his wooden desk.

Finally he looked up, his face hardened. "Savage continues to meet savage, and you go on without a shepherd?" he said.

"Yes sir."

"And the governor has won the war?"

"No sir."

"I do not understand, Eaton. Five Crows, Young Chief, Stickus, Camaspello and Umhowlish are all north of the Columbia or west of the big bend. Who commanded four hundred Cayuse warriors?"

"I do not know. I saw only a dozen warriors, sir."

The major stared again at the letter on the desk. He picked it up and read it again. "It's madness to call a council," he said. "The term of the governor's militia will be up, and I cannot protect him. General Wool has ordered me not to encourage his military activities in any way, not to give him rations, ammunition, even a horse or wagon.

"I wish you had not left Fort Naches, Andrew. It is true, Owhi did not come in, but I found him at his fishing grounds, and he professed peace again. Have you been to *Pishpishaston*?"

"No sir."

"It is beyond question the greatest fishery I have seen, the richest in the world. Owhi had fair reason to fish there rather than on the Naches. Yet I had to hire the rancher Blair to interpret, and he disliked the Indians so openly I requested the services of Father Sidalia. You might confess to him, Andrew."

"The governor expects me, sir."

"I will send my reply with Jacobs. He has ridden to Olympia by every route possible, and his chances are better than yours."

I saw his logic but could not fathom where it left me.

"You are a civilian interpreter and can muster yourself out of the militia," said Wells. "Write your resignation, and I will send it with Jacobs along with my justification."

"Thank you, sir."

"The new Fort Walla Walla needs another interpreter. Father Sidalia will attend the construction of a chapel and one hundred other duties here. The Pacific Army will pay you five and one-half dollars per day, Kettle Falls dust."

"What about Kamiakin, sir?"

"He may be with the Palus on the Touchet or farther north."

"I know the way. I request duty with any company ordered to locate or parley with him, sir."

"Request denied. I will not send you or any other party into the nests of angry hornets." The major spread his palm upon the table, and his bullet-eyes gripped me, narrow, suddenly dry and sky-like and scintillating, his face still sun-tough, bronze, smooth as a gun-bore, new white hairs lacing his thin blond thatch. ""Listen, Eaton, I expect barbarous acts from Indians, yet now white hands are stained with innocent blood, and President Pierce must face the consequences of his appointment. Congress must hold a full investigation, the Whigs especially."

"Yes sir."

"You will place your hand upon the Bible and swear an oath, Eaton. You will dictate every crime, name and incident you saw at Grande Ronde. I will witness your statements, and Sergeant Dole will record them. They will go directly to General Wool, and he will forward them to Secretary Davis, I trust."

"Yes sir."

"You are a courageous man, Eaton. It is one thing to stand in the face of the enemy, but to bare the truth before the One who metes out impartial justice, that is the only way America will make an honest territory out of this godforsaken wilderness."

I made statements for a day and a morning, sitting inside Wells' tent, the flaps closed, the sergeant dabbing his plume into his jar, the ink growing thick in the heat, flies buzzing and biting. Wells listened soberly, and his eyes turned to granite, his countenance suddenly corpse-like, his sweat smelling cold and clean even while the desert light poured unflinchingly through the canvas.

I signed my name, and we stepped out into the noonday glare, and Polka Dot Leggett yelled, hobbling swiftly toward me. "What kind of horseshit you been shoveling here, Eaton?" I buckled, and Wells flexed irritably beside me. "The Indians took seven thousand dollars from me!" cried Leggett. "What did you and that Indian-loving preacher do? Buy your skins with it?" His eyes bugged at Wells. "Did you search Eaton when he came in? I just saw Colonel Sheehan, and he said I was on Indian land when I was attacked, and I had no rights!"

Wells barked at the three blue-shirts escorting Leggett, and they closed around him.

"You have been issued a horse and ammunition, Mister Leggett," said Wells. "You are fortunate Colonel Sheehan did not arrest you."

"Arrest me?" Leggett lurched back from Wells, then forward again. "The colonel said that band with that squaw who talks so much English is waiting to come into council. He said no, you wouldn't send any soldiers to go after 'em. But you'll arrest a white citizen instead? A civilian?"

"You attacked an officer of the Pacific Army," said Wells.

"What officer?"

"The first chaplain in the entire United States Army."

"He's illegal here. The governor caught him planning with Kamiakin."

"The governor does not have the authority of martial law here, though he acts it," said Wells. "No one here is to backtalk or disrespect Father Sidalia in any manner."

Leggett guffawed and then thrust his chin at me. "What you got to say? Did the Indians cut your tongue? Did the major here vow you to keep quiet?"

"No," I said, "you know nothing about me, nothing about any squaw."

"See, he's a spy!" said Leggett. "He knows that talking squaw, Lalooh, Sparkling Water. And one a' my Kanakas seen him come up with an Indian while we was attacked. He done nothing to help us. He tried to sneak off."

"No, he did not sneak off. He is not a spy." Father Sidalia stepped around the corner of a tent, troops following, falling in sharply before the major. Leggett turned to the priest, lunging, and the escorts held him. "Mister Eaton speaks from darkness just as you do, Mister Leggett," said Sidalia. "He suffers a soul just as persecuted—as tormented—by the enemy as yours."

Leggett squirmed in the grasp of his escorts.

"Feel the slap, the sting against your cheek!" cried Sidalia. "Offer your other cheek! Forgive your brother not seven times, but seven times seventy!"

"Show me ye cheek, ye Injun lover!" said Leggett.

Sidalia smiled around at troops. "Indeed I behold the whiskey dealer, and I do not curse him. I bless him. I love him as all of us must love Kamiakin, Owhi, Quiltenenock, Five Crows, Umhowlish, Looking Glass—the squaw who grovels in the mud, who dances upon scalps—the brave who turns from one wife and takes another—who draws his bow and points his musket at innocents." A few troops moaned in dissent, and Sidalia calmly raised his chin, darkening his eyes seriously. "The Indians have practiced sorcery, and God has sent pestilence upon them. They have idolized demons, and He has taken away their lands. They have denied the fruits of his earth, and they are fading from it."

"Tell us, Father, does Jesus weep for the punished?" said Wells, his eyes suddenly ardent.

"Indeed, you saw the cross upon the moon," said Sidalia.

"Yes sir!" cried a soldier.

"As plain as day, sir!"

"It lasted until dawn, sir!"

"I felt it upon my cheeks, sir!"

"And in my heart, sir!"

"You're ruled by fools, all of you!" Leggett bucked amid his escorts, their hands slipping from his sweaty shirt, clutching him again. "You been around since the rivers opened up this spring, and all you done is graze grass! You're protecting the land, and you can't even settle on it!"

The escorts pulled at Leggett, and he lunged at Sidalia, was tripped, fell forward, and two more guards jumped on, and then the troops dragged Leggett between tents, and Wells and I followed, and Leggett howled and cussed, and I listened for her name, what else he might know about her, but he fell to mocking the soldiers' eyesight, their mothers and sisters. They got him past the tent-rows, pulled him up, whirled him and thrust him toward the guardhouse—one bad soldier hung from a scaffold by his thumbs, and another was strapped to the rim of a wagon wheel, his limbs stretched to their limits, his crotch rammed against the hub.

Leggett flexed his arms, stepping free from his escorts, and he dusted himself, wiping off the feel of their hands, not looking back, and he shuffled slowly toward the south line of the fort, fixing the knot of his neck scarf, hiding his hobble. He walked lazily past a sergeant and three more guards, and he climbed onto an old, tired-looking mare, and then he plodded away along Mill Creek, his mare so unhurried she kicked up no dust, his posture so unconcerned I nearly loved an enemy the way Sidalia had instructed.

"Good riddance," I said.

"How did you find my brandy, Eaton?" asked Wells.

"First rate, sir."

"Well, now they'll be less of it."

The Kanakas stayed. They built a chapel, and as the days grew hotter, Sidalia shunned me icily, and I returned the favor. I sat every day beneath a tarpaulin stretched between Wells' new cabin and Sheehan's, and I attended the army's four-columned ledger book, a dictionary, the first column English, the second Yakama (Sahaptin), the third Nez Perce (Sahaptin), the fourth Sinkiuse (Salish).

"Spring," said the first column; "*Wawáxm*," said the next, Lalooh's voice. "*Wawach*," said the third, her voice again—softly, slowly, patiently beside my ear, her gaze silent and wide as I remembered it at Ahtanum as she had waited for me to repeat each word after she had spoken it, Sidalia sitting on a mat with us in the shade of his cabin, dictating the spelling and accent marks in English.

When I finished the new dictionary, Sidalia would add the Salish and check my Sahaptin—*correct and teach* it to me, Wells had said! I had felt the order foul the moment he spoke it, and I continued to feel it so.

And one evening I closed the dictionary after retreat, and a mandolin twanged beyond the row of officers' cabins. The sound came from the chapel, a new instrument, and I walked over, and Sidalia plucked the strings outside, swaying easefully before Kanakas and troops sitting on gunnysacks, a shrine behind him, a Madonna, seven arrows stuck in her heart. He sang of the Assumption, the disciples at Mary's tomb, her body rising, and I wondered why I listened. I headed to the stables, feeling behind me only the butte where Sidalia and I had arrived, the glaring-bouncing shimmer reflecting from it, the gulches winding backward past Dry Creek to Quiltenenock's camp. But the camp would be empty now. Quiltenenock would have gone north up the Columbia to the old Sinkiuse sites, and the Yakama would have gone into high country, the braves hunting sheep and elk, the squaws picking *wiwlúwiwlu*.

"I leave before reveille tomorrow," I said to the stable clerk, and I went into the barn and cleaned and oiled my reins and saddle, tested the wood in the tree and stirrups, checked my blankets, extra horseshoes, bags, and I walked my gray to the creek and watered and combed her, washed and rubbed her legs, found the cuts from devil's club completely healed.

Lalooh, sweet Lalooh! Sweet as wiwlúwiwlu! *I left the governor at Grande Ronde. I left the army at the new fort. I started out for your huckleberry camp, hoping to find you drying* wiwlúwiwlu *in the sun, grinding them into your cakes with salmon oil, not on your way to the new council.*

I am still waiting, Lalooh. If your people do not take my gold and my horse, I am ashamed. If your people do not kill me, I am ashamed.

I listed the crimes at Grande Ronde, Lalooh. Major Wells will send the paper to the Great Father and Congress, and they will see the governor is bad, and his treaty is bad.

I do not wish to lie to you, Lalooh. My people tell so many lies they would tangle your itita'mat *forever. But I disputed the lies about Grande Ronde, so you can once again raise your face and look at me, so you and your people can once again have their lands. I think the Great Father will order a new treaty made by a different white chief.*

Listen, Lalooh! The chiefs must council without you. The whites know you—Polka Dot Leggett, Trader Purcell, Governor Rotten Wind, Major Wells, Bloody Beard and others. You must wait until the Great Father learns of Grande Ronde and names a new governor, then you can council again with the whites.

I knelt by my gray and picked up a hoof, looking for rot. A horse blew wearily behind me—Sidalia hurried to the bank, leading a tottering mount, the strawberry roan of One-armed Jacobs. He posted her a few steps up the creek, hung a nosebag of oats and hustled my way, glancing furtively at other troops watering mounts, beckoning me close, curling a finger.

I put down the hoof, picked up another, eyed it.

"Do not cling to your self with such stubborn determination," Sidalia said. "I will confess you here, baptize you here."

I glowered, studying the hoof.

"A demon inside me?" said Sidalia. "Posh! I just heard a voice. Mary spoke. I heard her from above—you see only your own wickedness, Eaton! Your lust! Your failures at Dry Creek and Grande Ronde! But Mary speaks only with love!"

I trimmed the hoof, thinking I might apologize. *But sometimes the black robe has his own devil inside him, and he does not know how to speak about beasts and farming.* I had forgotten I had said and meant it.

"You know hostiles might attack any day, and you can lose your soul forever," said Sidalia. "You know how serious your sins are. You know you must renounce them."

I watched my blade. "I have."

"You confessed only to the savage. You will merely remain savage."

I put down the hoof, my knife away. I felt no apology.

"You know there are only two loves in this world," said Sidalia. "There is the love of self which leads to the renunciation of God. And there is the love of God which leads to the renunciation of your self. You must choose."

I pulled my gray away by his snaffle, making toward the stable, and

Sidalia shook his head sorrowfully. "Wells sent me," he said. "He wants you immediately."

I reported to Wells directly, and he was at his desk, folding a dispatch into a tin box, and Jacobs sat bow-legged on a chair well behind him, resting in a corner, shoveling food one-handedly into his mouth, his hair and beard haggard and dusty from a weeks' riding, sweaty rings swollen around sunburned eyes.

Colonels, lieutenants and Sidalia came in, and Wells read a letter from the governor.

"My honorable Major Edward Wells—

"Where have you gained your reports of Grande Ronde? What traitors have given you such false and fabricated accounts?

"I do not propose to punish or exterminate any Indians but those clearly proven as the chief instigators of the war. History will present two crucial facts: the army has harbored and freed chiefs responsible for murder, yet not one of the thousand citizen volunteers who have served the Washington Militia during the past six months has injured the person or property of a single friendly or innocent Indian.

"The interior is not closed to white settlement. The Act of Congress, approved Sept. 27, 1850, entitled 'An act creating the office of the Surveyor General of public lands in Oregon etc.' and Acts of Feb. 14, 1853 and July 17, 1854, amended thereto, opened all the public domain in Washington Territory to settlers, they being required to certain acts of 'residence and cultivation.'

"It must certainly be doubted whether the commanding officer of a military department or district can legally exercise an authority which abrogates a statue of the United States and deprives white citizens of vested rights.

"It must also be certainly doubted that the separation of barbarous tribes from whites will improve the conditions of those tribes to husbandry, agriculture and Christian morality. The army will not civilize the Indians by idealizing the falsehoods of Kamiakin and other chiefs. It must take a more aggressive and manly course to prevent a resumption of the war. It must cease giving the Indians the impression the white nation is one of women.

"I left Olympia seven days past and will depart Fort Dalles tomorrow. I have mustered out all my companies save the one commanded by Colonel Benjamin

Nicholson, my courageous escort. While I hold council in the Walla Walla, your companies will naturally assume the protective duties of those recently departed.

"I will encamp on the new military reserve by the first of September. I am in need of an interpreter. The Indians, due to soreness resulting from their sound defeat at Grande Ronde, have grown leery of both Dominique Purcell and Andrew Eaton. I trust the army can provide an adequate man, and the territory will compensate."

Wells surveyed the countenance of Sidalia and every colonel and lieutenant. None stirred. All remained silent save Jacobs sipping, still replenishing his thirst, everyone's gaze secretly aimed at the tin box lying beside Wells' pipe.

"I told the governor this," said Wells. "It is unwise to open a council and seize hostile chiefs and transport them to trial during our unsettled state of Indian relations. Instead, he must pledge amnesty to chiefs and wait until the fort is fully constructed, and more companies arrive, perhaps next spring. And if he persists, he must not incite Indians against us by his presence on the military reserve. He and Nicholson's company must encamp at least ten miles away from our boundaries. I told him there is no extra interpreter here."

"Sir," said Sidalia, "I will go."

"You have duties here, Father Sidalia. The governor will arrest you."

"I am called, sir. Father Methode has been exiled at Kettle Falls ever since Ahtanum burned. He speaks Salish as well as Sahaptin. He can assume my duties very well here."

Wells lifted the tin box. "This goes immediately."

"I am called, I say," said Sidalia. "I know the back way through Dry Creek. It has been proven the Indians will show me restraint."

"Very well, you will be on loan from the war department, outside the jurisdiction of any of the governor's mandates."

"I am ruled only by God, Major, but very well, as you say."

"Godspeed to you."

"Ho!" said Colonel Sheehan.

"Yes, Godspeed!" said others.

Wells stood and handed Sidalia the box. "Do not give the governor any false hope, Father. I expect General Wool will only grow firmer when the *Eleanor Scott* arrives at San Francisco, and he reads testimony about Grande Ronde."

"The *Eleanor Scott!*" Jacobs sat up suddenly, his chair banging the wall. "She sank, sir, smashed to bits off **Cape Blanco**! Nothing was recovered!"

And so I stayed and gave testimony again.

And I sat a fortnight later beneath a council arbor as Looking Glass unrolled an elk-skin map, his forehead smeared red, tippets of scalps, ears and fingers hanging from his hair, hundreds of Nez Perce warriors on mounts outside the freshly-sawed logs of the stockade.

"These are our lands," said Looking Glass. "We have ordered all whites off them. We will not council with Rotten Wind. We are waiting for the army to hang him."

"My mission here is pacific," I said, translating for Wells. "I have not come to fight you but to live among you."

"The Americans hanged Cayuse when they killed the reverend and his wife and took white women," said Looking Glass. "They hanged Yakama and Klickitat when they attacked the Cascades. Tell me, when will you hang Rotten Wind? And Bloody Beard? Trader Purcell? And the Lanky One, Kills Many Squaws?"

"I can tell you only that General Wool has ordered me to arrest the governor if he repeats his acts here," said Wells.

"The governor is encamped on Wallawalla land," said Looking Glass. "When will you remove him?"

"I cannot remove him," said Wells. "I sent a message to the Great Father, and it was lost upon the sea."

The piercing-blue bullet-eyes met swollen-impenetrable brown, and Wells looked down and studied the elk-skin as muskets popped from the grasses out by the buttes, rifles clapped, and warriors screamed and rode mock-charges, their horses and near-naked bodies streaked and zigzagged amid dust clouds, festooned with war-bonnets and streamers, painted shields and lances.

"These were our lands a long time before the Great Father sent Captain Lewis and Captain Clark, before we showed them the way to the Columbia and wintered their horses," said Looking Glass. "The treaty cannot take our lands away. Lawyer knew nothing when he signed it. I am asking a plain question.

Will you give us back our lands? That is what troubles us, what we want to hear about. I ask plainly to have a plain answer."

"The Great Father will decide about the treaty," said Wells.

I translated, and a tall-young brave sitting with Looking Glass and the other chiefs glared crossly at me, his nose flaring, delicately-bridged, his chest deep and strong like Nammakin's, his lips as thin and fine as Lalooh's. "When you get the last word with an echo, you will get the last word with the Great Father," said the brave, who seemed no older than I, his eyes dark and smooth, as liquidly sagacious as a cougar's who reclined upon a ledge, watching a herd of pronghorns. "I am Thunder Rolling in the Mountains," he said. "Joseph. Our fathers taught us laws which were taught by their fathers. They were good laws. They told us to treat all men as they treated us—never be the first to break a bargain—it is a disgrace to lie. They taught us that white chiefs have the same power over their men as red chiefs—if bad whites do wicked things, their chiefs have the power to punish and stop them. Thus the white chiefs at Grande Ronde are responsible for all the lives taken there, not just those they themselves killed.

"Long Elk's life was worth more than the entire Grande Ronde Valley, more than the entire world. Panther's life was worth the same. The Cayuse are our brothers, and the values of their lives cannot be told. Since my brothers' lives were taken there, and the earth drank their blood, the valley is more sacred to us than ever before. We claim the valley for all the lives taken there. The Nez Perce and Cayuse have hunted and fished and gathered roots there forever, and now the whites will stay out of it forever."

Looking Glass rolled up the elk-skin. "When the major finds his heart free again, no longer stolen by General Wool and the Great Father, he can bring us Rotten Wind. We will stand him before the Cayuse. We will judge him by the laws passed down to us.

"Do away with all white treaties. Give us back our lands. Let no white man come into our country, and there will be peace. If not, then we will fight."

The Nez Perce refused provisions, a feast, a closing smoke. They rode south toward the governor, and Wells paced that evening along Mill Creek, casting a fishing rod recently delivered by Jacobs, shipped from Vermont. The major flicked his pole and watched his fly snap through clouds of bugs, the rod whistling, his wrist-strokes as firm and sure as the dispatch he dictated to me. *"I am having a fine time, Governor, catching trout and cleaning my shotgun, getting ready to hunt grouse. You can serve Washington Territory by pursuing the same pleasures. You might cancel your council, or if you have commenced it, adjourn it.*

"Looking Glass was here today, and he claimed more than half the Nez Perce nation hostile, unwilling to obey the treaty, anxious to see you hanged. I believe his party is riding your way and may join the Cayuse and other tribes to avenge Grande Ronde.

"I do not have sufficient troops to protect both you and Fort Walla Walla, thus I suggest you feign a reason to return to Olympia. If you find the way to the Columbia too hazardous, you can perhaps make it here via Dry Creek. But if you allow yourself the fort's shelter, you must not attribute the suggestion to me. You must keep its source a secret to yourself."

Wells jerked his fly viciously from a sweep of branch-tangles. He spat distastefully. He signed the dispatch, and I carried it toward Jacobs, proceeding up the creek toward the strawberry roan standing with other mounts around a mosquito fire.

A moan sounded loudly behind a big cottonwood, Jacobs gasped painfully. He rose from squatting, and he staggered, wincing, and he saw the tin box in my hand and gave me a quick-sweaty glance and ducked behind the tree again. He discharged noisily, splashing, crying out again, and then he hit the ground, buckling his knees, a leaf in hand, and he writhed in his excrement, grabbing a leg, and I reached down, and he looked at me large-eyed, feverish and pale, and I stopped.

"Cramps," he said. "I'm almost done, and then I'll saddle up."

I nodded agreeably and then shot off, trembling, silencing a shout for Wells as I returned to him.

"Did you touch him?" asked Wells. "Is it on your boots?"

"No sir."

"Did you breathe it?"

"I kept away, sir."

"It may not be what we think."

"No, sir, but I will take the dispatch myself. You still have Father Methode to translate."

Wells looked up the creek and seemed to see every nation of savages advance at once. He bullied away the worry on his face. "Jacobs rode via Dry Creek yesterday," he said. "Don't drink from it. Avoid any water you don't absolutely need. Make sure you dip your cup deep. Don't skim the surface."

"Yes sir."

"You must consider Kamiakin, the revengeful nature of all Indians. I pray they have not put some poison into our streams."

I fought a dark mood of doom, galloping from the stable on my bay, driving my gray before me as two troops lifted Jacobs from beside the creek and slid him on a litter onto a wagon-bed. I had made acquaintance enough with cholera on our way west—the poor-punished souls wasted beside the road, lying on the ground or sitting against some tree, abandoned by their trains, reduced to begging—bundles of their discarded clothes reeking of diarrhea—bloated corpses swarming with buzzards—grave after grave after grave.

I gained the top of the sappers' butte and turned and watched Jacobs' wagon moving toward the farthest hospital tent, quarantine, and I knew Doc Hammond would give Jacobs all the tinctures of laudanum he needed, pepper and camphor, mustard plasters, and I thought Jacobs would lick it if anyone could. He ate rattlesnakes when he rode express. He skinned them and ran a stick through and roasted them, and I figured he had eaten one that had bitten itself while being clubbed, and he had earned his trouble that way.

His wagon rolled into shadow, and I tarried, not knowing why. Campfires smoked peacefully amid rows of tents, guards rode punctiliously along picketed horses, and the evening light poured streaks above stream-mist and the stockade and up the slope below me, the grasses tingeing yellow, beaten down by the Nez Perce maneuvers, smelling sweet like chaff and hay and manure. The Nez Perce trail was clear. They had not approached the fort by climbing the east side of the sappers' butte as Sidalia and I had when we had arrived. They had ridden in from the north, maybe after consulting with Kamiakin, and they had left along Mill Creek like Leggett.

The night promised coolness, maybe frost, and my gray stared at me, perking her ears, blowing wisps of vapor. She did not understand my hesitation either. She waited dutifully, swaying toward a trace left by Jacobs, and then

I felt a piece of his courage, and I thought of Lalooh, and my chest swelled against my uniform blouse, and I snapped my quirt, a strength finally tingling and pounding through every inch of me again.

The moon lit the gulches, nearly full for the second time since Sidalia's cross, and owls moaned, whistling, and coyotes yapped, and prickly pears threw shadows, and my gray veered, kicking at them, scattering stone and clay, and my bay kept pulling hard, trying to follow her, and when we came to Dry Creek, the defile densely dark, I thought watering would be all right. I dismounted and listened. Dry Creek roared laughing off the rock, not dry at all. The Blues still melted up high, and I saw Wells was wrong, the Indians had not poisoned the water. Dry Creek ran too deep and fast, and cholera did not come from medicine men anyway. It came from nowhere—as if God really looked down upon us and delivered it just as He had delivered the Flood.

I picketed the horses and walked slowly through the defile, smelling creosote bushes up on rock, flinty like the first taste of a thunderhead, sharp like the last fumes of a sulfur match, and then the bottoms opened, and I followed Jacobs' trace, boot-prints so clear they seemed to rise from the powdery-gray ground. They ended at a jam of storm debris, and I knelt and looked into the sticks and logs and mud, smelling ashes, burned bones, burned lodge-skins, burned buffalo robes. I clasped my hands and wanted to pray. I thought for a prayer, and none came, but something looked down—a ledge loomed above cottonwood-crowns, its moon shadow dark to the rim, Narcisse's pinnacle-rock beyond it.

The squaw crawled, knocking sticks, scraping her moccasin, gripping her pregnancy belt. "Eaton! Tie off her foot!" My knees knelt cold on snow, her blood ran warm on my hands, she stared at my fingers silently, hatefully.

The moon pounded down, pouring cold beams, watching me through deep-gray eye-sockets. Lalooh! I knew she would be here, sitting as if by the bone-white cottonwood.

"I first saw the friendlies from that ledge, Lalooh, and I did not think fast enough!"

The moon prickled into my cheeks and throat, and I knew I engaged in tomfoolery, clung to it with stubborn determination.

The creek quieted, and something slapped from above, the slightest moist sound—the echo of a splash?

Something licked something. Licked and licked and stopped.

A wolf sat up on her rump between the ledge and Narcisse's rock, narrowing her ears, pointing her snout at me, her eyes shiny and broad. She licked her ruff, ash-colored in the moonlight, her breast lighter, almost snowy. She was calm in a way I did not like. I drew and cocked my pistol, and she raised her snout and gave a long-drawn howl, and barks started up on the plain, a pack behind her, and she looked down again, raising her rump, standing on all fours—her heart an easy shot—which hostiles would hear for miles.

The barks behind her increased, and I squatted slowly and clawed into the soil, and she wagged her snout and sniffed, lifting lips from teeth, her stare pouring hot through my brow. I gripped a stone. I slowly stood. I hurled the stone—it thumped the ledge and careened, and she jumped back, buoyant as a fox, younger than I thought, and I slowly bent as if for another stone. I turned and walked out.

My gray and bay neighed, tugging their lines, and I yanked the picket-pins, thankful I had driven them deep, and I slung myself onto my bay, and she flew down the next gulch, my thorn-wary gray following without a line, then passing us at a straight gallop, the prickly pear be damned.

The gulch turned into several others, and the trail wound up a long hill, broadening into a swath of unshod hooves and wagon ruts, the fresh tracks of masses of Indians. The trail turned dark beneath oaks, black as a root cellar, but my mounts sensed herds ahead, sped on, lathered, and I smelled more ash, tasted it, and we came out to a milky-blue blaze, the moon hanging across a valley, the ground directly before us smoldering, foggy with smoke. Little pockets of flames winked below us, descending the crown of a butte, and my bay pulled up, and my gray trotted back toward the oaks and stood waiting again.

Someone wept below, wailing. An Indian. He moaned as if he had the cramps—charred stems of grasses stretched all the way left and right, and I thought the cholera had visited a camp or two or worse, and remains had been burned, and the council grounds was near.

Braves mumbled guttural grunts, their steps thudding heavily uphill.

"*Lolo!*" I called. *Here!* "*Sikh!*" *A friend!*

A big warrior climbed broadly through the smoke, the hood of his robe down—Kamiakin, two braves coming behind him, logs on their shoulders, a body slung inside a blanket between them.

"*Ty'ee,*" I said. *Chief.*

Kamiakin slowed painstakingly, eyeing me, and he beckoned me down, and I consented. I nodded a question at the blanket, and a squaw spoke, laying fingers across my hand. "*Sikh pel'ton.*" *Friend a fool.* Lalooh stood beside me, staring unblinking, her eyes urgently wide, and I gaped, disbelieving, and she gripped my bay's reins and swung rapidly, leading both horses away.

Kamiakin beckoned again, and two braves carried the body into the darkness of the oaks, and we followed, and torches approached—Nammakin, Owhi, Skloom, Blue Hawk, Stickus, other war chiefs.

The two braves lowered and opened the blanket, and Nammakin moved a torch above a corpse mercilessly burned, ruthlessly blistered, an ivory crucifix blackened and burned into the chest-bone, a little tin box melted against a wrist.

"Almcotty saw Father Sidalia from the sky!" Lalooh stepped into the torchlight, staring fully at me again, her eyes flashing amid flaring flames. "Almcotty looked down and saw a rattlesnake blinded by the black gown's whip! He put the snake in the black gown's mind, and the black gown rode straight into Blue Hawk's fire!"

Some of the war chiefs yipped and chattered among themselves, grinning viciously in the fiery dark, and then Kamiakin and Blue Hawk squatted heavily by Sidalia's body, quietly, and the rest of the Indians followed suit.

Blue Hawk spoke to me through Lalooh, grizzly claws painted on his cheeks. "You must talk with us, must listen like a bird to his brother. Your hair must be straight this time, not crooked. How many blue-shirts are coming behind you?"

"None," I said.

"Your hair is crooked," said Nammakin.

"No, Rotten Wind and Major Wells are jealous chiefs," said Kamiakin. "They do not talk the same. They do not fight or believe the same."

"Is this so?" Lalooh's stare penetrated me, and I nodded yes.

"The Cayuse did not kill the black gown," said Blue Hawk.

"We fired the grasses around Rotten Wind, so his horses would grow hungry, and he would go away," said Stickus.

"We fired the grasses for Panther and Long Elk," said Blue Hawk, and he recited name after name, Cayuse after Cayuse killed at Grande Ronde. "We are sorry for the priest, but he had a snake in his mind. He rode his roan across coals, and he was thrown."

"I want to see his back," I said.

Braves rolled him, skin tore off in patches. I saw neither bullet hole nor stab mark. "The death will anger the governor," I said.

"You must take the body down to Rotten Wind," said Kamiakin. "Tell him he was wrong to send the black robe into the fire, and he will only be right when he tosses the treaty away into flames. Tell him we will not come to his council, and we will not be killed like Peopeomoxmox. Tell him I made a mark of friendship only on the treaty. I did not make a mark to give away all the Indians' lands."

"Lalooh must leave," I said. "All squaws and children must."

"You talk to us like Rotten Wind," said Nammakin. "You order us."

He and Kamiakin rose with Owhi and Blue Hawk. They bent and wrapped the blanket around the body again, and Kamiakin sang a spirit song— he had regained his power. He clearly seemed the Yakama leader again. He quieted, and the two braves stepped forward and lifted the corpse again. They carried it through the oaks, and the sheen of their long dark hair shone beneath blue-gnarled branches, and Lalooh and the others fell behind without further ceremony.

We reached my mounts freshly combed in the dawn-glow, standing posted and waiting on the trail, looking fed and watered, my rifle still in its saddle holster, my packs remaining in perfect order, magpies jabbering, criers singing in nearby camps in several Indian languages.

The braves lashed the corpse to my bay, and I walked my mounts down along the edge of the ashes, feeling hurry a sudden enemy, the governor an old reluctance, the horses' steps as unwilling as my own. Stream-mist and smoke lingered in the valley, and a bugler played stable call—though the governor's herd would breakfast only on contract hay and oats, encamped as he was in a little hole just in front of Mill Creek, backed by a bare-steep butte, circled by a small score of friendly lodges, and flanked by hostile lodges stretching upstream and down, how many hundreds or thousands I dared not think.

A friendly Nez Perce stood boldly from his picket post, seeing my uniform, then the body.

"Sidalia," I said, and the brave whirled, bolting amid lodges, and I waited outside the camp, and Lawyer and the governor came quickly, both riding bareback, Lawyer wearing a white man's blouse un-buttoned, the governor with Nez Perce sashes loosely looped around a trapper's shirt—each man caught in the middle of dandying himself for the council day.

Lawyer led us around his camp and across the creek and up a draw that swung sharply north and then narrowed secretly, and we dismounted and climbed toward chuffing and clunking—two militiamen already shoveled through sediment, and Dominique stood by an old-silvered stump, clasping a Bible two-handedly, and Major Nicholson and Lieutenant-major Taylor kept watch behind him, dressed in furs and buckskins like the governor, no longer in kepis and military jackets.

Dominique came stolidly to me, embraced me briefly, glanced at me furtively—a momentary glint of trust, a dismissal of the nonsense ahead.

He and I lowered the corpse and opened the blanket, and Taylor and Nicholson knelt and pored over it stern-eyed.

"Did you see his horse, Eaton?" said Taylor. "Exactly where he fell?"

"No," I said.

"Then you do not really know how he died, or who killed him," said Nicholson.

He and Taylor stood huffily. "I saw Father Sidalia leave," said Taylor. "He did not ride toward the fire."

"I sent him to Wells *because* of the fire," said the governor.

"Someone chased Father Sidalia into it—the Cayuse!" said Nicholson. "Ordered by Kamiakin!"

Taylor glared at me. "They let Sidalia burn, but they let you live."

"Why?" said Nicholson.

"That blue shirt, that blue uniform," said Taylor. "Because they know Eaton is not brave enough to shoot an Indian."

I stood below them, feeling my head hang, and I disliked their accusing looks as much as the brazen calm of the she-wolf, the governor hot and quiet beside me, Lawyer now inspecting the body, coolly fingering the disfigured crucifix.

The Nez Perce chief stood perplexed. "Where is Jacobs?"

"He got the cramps," I said, and I bulleted a look smugly at Taylor. "Major Wells thought he might have dipped his cup too deep at Dry Creek."

Taylor and Nicholson snickered, and Dominique drew the Bible to his chest, his lips stubbornly pinched. He steadied his dismay and looked at me with open alarm. "You are certain about Jacobs?"

"No, but he could not stop discharging himself," I said. "He was in quarantine when I left."

Dominique looked at the governor with a question.

"I shall announce the postponement, and we shall march to Wells regardless," said the governor. "The council will resume at the fort, whatever the consequence to my personal safety. We will not be cowed by hostile chiefs, a rumor of disease or the failure of an express. I called the council, and I will not dishonor Father Sidalia's sacrifice by closing it prematurely."

The two militiamen lowered Sidalia into the shallow grave.

"General Wool and Major Wells will claim Father Sidalia's death as my responsibility," said the governor. "Bishop Blanchet and Pope Pius will also blame me. But I trust He who holds the heart of every man has delivered the priest his reward, and He has spared many more of us than the savages would have."

Dominique opened the Bible, and we took off our hats and knelt: "In the sweat of thy face shalt thou eat bread, till thou returns unto the ground, for out of it wast thou taken, for dust thou art, and unto dust shalt thou return."

The governor ordered canteens stealthily filled, haversacks, saddlebags and cartridge boxes packed out of sight, tents ready to strike, saddles prepared, "a double quick" departure after his announcement. He called me into his tent and offered me bourbon, and I deferred and sat at his desk opposite him, my ears burning, my pluck too small to meet the occasion.

"I sent Pretty Jim with an express to Wells—on back trails to the west, not via Dry Creek," he said. "You will remain here to replace Father Sidalia." He drained his cup with two long drinks, his over-arching brow furrowing and beading sweat. "If you mention Dry Creek or the cholera again, you will be gagged. The troops must not fear the fort, Eaton. If you persist, you will be charged with the same crime as a coward who abandons his post. You will face a firing squad."

"I believe I answer to Wells, not the territory," I said.

"I remind you lives are at imminent risk, and I am not only the governor, but the Superintendent of Indian Affairs in Washington Territory, vested by federal authority." The governor drank again. "We will march up Mill Creek and reach the fort *openly* under Major Wells' invitation. I told Wells I refuse to keep his wisdom clandestine, and history will decorate him for defying Wool."

"None of the chiefs I saw this morning will council with you," I said. "They claim they did not sign the treaty to give away their lands."

"They are either lying, or the interpreters at the first council failed them— you yourself, Eaton. You point out the deficiencies of your own efforts."

The governor handed me the journal of the new council, previously kept by Sidalia, and then he rose, pouring himself more bourbon.

We proceeded with Dominique and Lawyer toward the arbor and the flag, all of us unarmed, our perimeter thickly picketed with the gamest men from the governor's seventy troops and Lawyer's fifty warriors— the arbor itself to be guarded by Nicholson, Taylor, Farveaux and Northcroft—pistols hidden beneath their coats to meet the prospect of firearms and knives beneath the robes of chiefs.

"Go slow with the chiefs today," Dominique said to the governor. "Let them carry on. Give Pretty Jim time to reach Wells and Wells time to send Dragoons and his twelve-pounders."

"I will count on Pretty Jim, not Wells," said the governor. "You saw his express—he sounds like an old woman who wants to stay home and knit."

"Ho, look here!" A bellowing voice hailed us from the creek. Willows waved and cracked, and Charles Leggett pushed out, the narrow-yellow leaves raining on him. He led two mules strapped with wooden crates stamped **Bibles, Shakespeare, Sir Walter Scott**. His hobble was gone, and he looked at me expeditiously, suggesting a mountain of forgiveness, the necessity of our situation. He smiled grandly at the governor, and we turned down the bank to him, and Leggett drew a spear-point knife and pried open a crate—Boston breechloaders were stacked inside—spanking new, brass hammers glittering as the sun burned off the mist, the gunstocks cherry-toned, beautifully grained. "A-hundred of 'em," said Leggett.

The governor handed him a pocket flask, and Leggett swigged heartily.

"Distribute them to the pickets first, then the remainder of my troops, then to Spotted Eagle, war chief of Lawyer," said the governor. "Leave one for Dominique and myself."

"And Andrew," said Dominique.

"Yes, I do not begrudge it," said the governor. "But he must relinquish it when he returns to Wells, or pay the territory in gold."

He led us jauntily up the bank, a spare-little bull of a man chugging forward with direct vigor, suddenly four steps ahead, private and silent with his own contemplations.

"You see the grasses burned all around us!" said the governor. "You see how the Cayuse have committed another crime! How the Cayuse have left me with only Master Purcell to translate! Nothing to feed my horses! But God has taught me to love the Indians, and I am here to make a good peace in spite of a few bad braves!"

A handful of chiefs sat before many rows of empty benches—Eagle from the Light, three Nez Perce sub-chiefs, an Umatilla chief, a Wallawalla chief, a Klickitat chief—Quiltenenock on the front bench—Lalooh high-chinned beside him, wearing a shredded sage-bark dress, her braids greased green with fir scent.

Dominique spoke the governor's words, wearing a Hudson's Bay frock coat, a collar broad and white as in the days when Indians and whites traded peacefully.

Lalooh repeated his Nez Perce dialect to Quiltenenock, and the Sinkiuse chief signed *yes, he understood*— his face was unpainted, his hair-part was combed handsomely with white clay, his upper lip was pierced primitively with a beaded bone, his grip tightly clutched his yellowed letter from Sidalia.

"I am here to smoke with you!" said the governor.

Lawyer lit a pipe with a stem carved with heaven's rays, a dove and cross, the archangel Gabriel, heads and horns of an antelope, elk, buffalo.

Each chief eyed it circumspectly. Each took a long time to smoke and pass it, and Lalooh sat with her hands in her lap, slowly eyeing my plume and soldier's shirt, then staring squarely into my gaze, her copper stare deepening, holding I knew not what in their depths anymore. Her cheeks arched tautly, thinly now, and she set her lips resolutely, and a shimmer rose around her head, wreathed in swirling smoke, and I wondered what it was. The shimmer played about her skin and hair, brightening them, glistening off the bones and shells of her necklace, sliding up the hollow of her throat as she coolly raised her chin, studying each of us, her shredded-sage dress making the slightest-pale rustling. The shimmer seemed sunlight itself, yet no chief seemed to see it. No one else in our party looked at it. She herself did not seem to know the strange light that glowed around her.

"Who wishes to speak?" said Dominique.

"Quiltenenock, chief of the Sinkiuse," said Lalooh. "He did not sign the treaty, yet the treaty took away the Sinkiuse land. Kamiakin signed the treaty, but he himself says he is not the Sinkiuse chief. The Sinkiuse chief is Quiltenenock."

"Go on," said Dominique.

"We are sorry the black gown died yesterday," said Lalooh. "He was a good friend, but he can no longer tell the governor how the Sinkiuse have helped whites. But Quiltenenock has a letter from the black gown, and it says so."

The governor rose again: "I regret the body that Kamiakin sent to us this morning. It is white, but I am not sure it belongs to the priest. It may be a miner or a soldier killed by Kamiakin, but Kamiakin is not here to say. He is hiding in the buttes."

"But Quiltenenock is not hiding." Quiltenenock spoke, Lalooh translated. "Quiltenenock has never hidden. He was not at the council when Kamiakin signed the treaty. He was not invited. He wishes to meet the governor and change the lines of the treaty."

The governor paced before the Indian benches, stopped, smiled amicably down at the Sinkiuse chief. "Quiltene—!" He wriggled his lips, struggling with Salish sounds. "Quiltomee! Who is Quiltomee? Who are the Sinkiuse?"

He looked at Lawyer, and Lawyer rose, opened the treaty, read from the foolscap, "It is distinctly understood and agreed that at the time of the conclusion of this treaty Kamiakin is the duly elected and authorized head of the confederated tribes and bands aforesaid, styled the Yakama nation, and is recognized by them and by the commissioners on the part of the United States holding the treaty."

"Kamiakin marked the treaty, and his mark cannot be changed simply by a letter from Father Sidalia," said the governor, Dominique translating. "The law is made by the Great Father in Washington, and I cannot change it. I stand here for the Great Father, and my orders are plain, and I will execute them. I will not meet with Quiltomee. I must go find better grass."

Lalooh spoke the words into Quiltenenock's ear, and the chief clouded his eyes. Lawyer rose and read again, "The aforesaid confederated tribes and bands of Indians acknowledge their dependence upon the government of the United States, and promise to be friendly with all citizens thereof, and pledge themselves to commit no depredations upon the property of such citizens... And the said confederated tribes of the bands of the Indians agree not to conceal offenders against the laws of the United States, but deliver them up to the authorities for trial."

"Tell me, Quiltomee," said the governor, "where are Skistymay, Nammakin and the other braves who attacked Charles Leggett? Will Quiltomee bring them in, so they can face justice?"

Quiltenenock glowered at the governor, listening to Lalooh once more. The governor frowned down at Lalooh. "Where are the squaws who passed guns?" Lalooh held her head high, the governor went on. "Will Quiltomee bring in the squaws? Will he bring in Kamiakin? Will he show America he can meet the terms of the treaty? No, he will not!" The governor clasped his hands, swaying, tottering, smiling, looking down at the chief. "The Great Father is honorable, and I am honorable. I invited Indians to this council under safe conduct. Thus you were safe in coming. Thus you will be safe in going. But if hostiles want peace, I know only one way. They must give up their arms and submit to the mercy and justice of the Territory of Washington. If friendlies want peace, I know only one way. They must prove they have not attacked whites, and they must bring in all the hostile chiefs who have broken the law."

Quiltenenock and Lalooh rose, looking past the governor at me. "Andrew, can you speak?" said Lalooh. "Can you be our friend? Can you tell us what words will make the governor open his ears?"

I scribbled her questions in the journal, feeling her watching. "You have already spoken them," I said. "I know no other words."

"The black gown has a dead snake rotting in his mind!" Quiltenenock rose abruptly. "The governor has a snake rotten and dead in his mind! Master Purcell has one! Andrew Eaton has one!

"All people and animals will be gone! Creation overthrown! Buffalo all gone! Elk and deer fenced! Eagles caged! All our freedom gone, all our happiness broken! Earth will be broken open everywhere! Nature will be smoothed and straightened like a gun barrel! All flowers will look down weeping! The forests will melt! The rivers will be held back! They will dry up! The salmon will dry up! They will no longer feed the tribes!"

Lalooh translated, standing beside Quiltenenock, and the governor screwed up his eyes, irritated, and something rustled behind him, cloth and steel. Lalooh glared at Taylor as he drew his pistol's handle from his coat. "I, Lalooh, have dreamt about this one!" she cried. "He climbed upon an Indian woman at Dry Creek while that one"—she looked my way—"held a gun to her." She looked at Taylor again. "This one beat her brutally while he took her, in such a fashion to condemn every white on our land!" She looked at Dominique. "This one had a son who killed the woman brutally with a stick, in such a fashion to condemn every white here today!" She looked at the governor, Nicholson, Taylor again. "These men killed Indian women, children, old men, old women at Grande Ronde! They trampled them with horses! They shot them while they fled and hid inside their lodges! They shot them while they bathed in sulfur water, bothering no one, while they merely cleaned themselves, warming their bones!" She looked at Taylor, Farveaux, Northcroft. "These men cut up Indian women like white women cut potatoes!" She looked at the governor again. "This one blames the Cayuse! He blames Kamiakin! But we call him Rotten Wind! He speaks his words, and we smell the snake decaying inside him! It swells and rots inside his mind! It drips pus and dries to a stench inside his heart!"

"Nawit'ka!" said Quiltenenock. Yes indeed! "We wish no blood today, no battle, but Rotten Wind has spoken to the Sinkiuse like worms! He has seen the

Sinkiuse chief and remained blind! He has heard the Sinkiuse chief and grown deaf!

"Skistymay dreamt—a tanager in hailstones! Nammakin dreamt—an eagle in a landslide! They know no bullets will touch them today!"

Lalooh translated, and the governor bugged his eyes around, keeping Nicholson, Taylor and others from objecting with words or arms. "Council adjourned!" he said, and he pivoted and marched from the arbor, and we fell in behind him, the Indians lingering, standing amid the benches, grumbling low grunts, chattering heatedly behind us.

We proceeded in haste, troops collapsing canvas all around us, tossing saddles onto mounts, crates into wagons, and the governor suddenly limped, advancing his rupture-leg gingerly, pulling it in by jerks. He ordered us to the camp chairs behind his tent, and he sat drinking from his bourbon cup, biting away pain, and he glared at Taylor as the lieutenant-major pulled a flask partway out of a pocket. "No more for you!" The governor looked at Nicholson. "Take it from him—the pistol too!" Nicholson stood, and Taylor shrank, collapsing his long-lanky cheeks, letting his eyes droop like a hound after a whipping. "She is red, and you are white!" cried the governor. "Yet she made a fool of you!"

Taylor glared in retaliation. He pulled his flask all the way out. He uncorked it and refreshed himself generously, and Nicholson leaned before him, flexing an open hand over-patiently.

"Benjamin, Dominique!" said the governor. "Remove the drink and weapon! If Taylor cannot obey, tie him to that post over there!"

Taylor drank again and handed Nicholson his flask and pistol.

"The Indians are expected to speak the devil and pull weapons at peace councils!" said the governor. "We are expected to teach them dignity! I ought to hang you—if I could spare you, I would!"

"Their talk incited me, sir," said Taylor. "I lay my shame before you."

"Lay it before all of us!" said the governor. "Everyone might have been killed!"

"I think we are all right," said Dominique. "We might send Quiltenenock a message and tell him we will meet him at the fort. It will calm the Indians as we move, and you can change your mind later."

"I have never lied to an Indian, and I never will," said the governor.

"We must proceed as planned," said Nicholson. "Otherwise they will think we are afraid. They will smell our fear."

"We might remain here instead," said Dominique. "The Nez Perce can take our stock out to grass and bring them back in." Lawyer nodded, and Dominique went on. "We can wait until nightfall—until we know if Pretty Jim got through, and Wells is coming. If we get no word, we can leave after midnight. The hostiles will wake tomorrow and find us gone."

"With the moon full?" said the governor. "And scouts on every eminence?"

"The Cayuse are trying their same old wickedness," said Nicholson. "They're closing us in before they attack—the sooner we fight them, the better. They will learn someday there can only be one result. The Cayuse will lose, and we will win."

"Quiltenenock is not Cayuse," said Dominique.

"Nor is he a party to the treaty," said the governor. He glared in disgust at Taylor again. "A pitiful squaw!" He winced and shook his head as if he disbelieved the immensity of the lieutenant-major's blunder.

We marched north in order of battle, our Boston breechloaders slung across our backs, Dominique cantering beside me, holding a flag of truce, glancing coolly askance at clusters of squaws standing by lodges, showing no hurry to pack or leave. We passed the last of the lodges, seeing no braves. We entered a basin, an open bowl, buttes on all sides, the creek a slither of s-curves, the valley mostly flat, the bunchgrass waving, making me uneasy.

Dust rose from a hillock halfway to the eastern buttes—four Indians approached on painted war ponies. They stopped about four rods from our line, swung and rode saucily beside us—Lalooh in her council dress, Quiltenenock, Skistymay and Nammakin stripped for battle, the first with bear fangs painted freshly on his cheeks, the next wearing his eagle plumes, the last in his wolf-head war cap, boasting a U.S. army rifle and cartridge belt, pumping his painted pole and charcoal-colored horsetail and scalp.

Dominique retrieved his gaze from the scalp. He swallowed his rage, I thought. He hurried me with a nod, and we pulled out of line, trotted beside it and reached the governor as Nicholson, Lawyer and Spotted Eagle drew beside him, Taylor hanging back a few horse-lengths.

Lalooh and the braves thundered away. They galloped along our front guard of Nez Perce, yelling, gesturing insults, stomping hooves, and a larger mass of dust billowed out on the hillock, thirty or forty Sinkiuse warriors spreading out toward both ends of our line.

"Halt!" cried the governor. "Halt and corral the wagons! Chain the wheels! Get the stock inside!"

Lalooh and the three braves returned, rearing before us, and the governor wriggled stiffly in his saddle, spun clumsily, shouted down the line, "Shackles!"

A teamster pulled out with a wagon equipped with chains and iron rings, and Quiltenenock tossed back his head, snarling, grinning.

"We do not want to fight Lawyer," said Lalooh. "No Nez Perce."

Lawyer took the truce-flag from Dominique and broke and waved it, and the Nez Perce turned horses toward the creek. They retreated across it, and Lalooh and the braves wheeled, galloping back up a gentle slope, and Taylor whipped his mount, breaking rank, riding after them.

"About face!" called the governor. "Hold your fire, Taylor!"

Taylor galloped on a tall-chestnut stallion, holding a breechloader at his waist, and the four Indians fanned out, seemingly unaware of him, and I packed a cartridge, tied it, bit the string, men all around me doing the same, dropping loads into breeches, cocking triggers.

"Nicholson, Leggett, skirmish order!" The governor pointed the two men and their squads left and right into grass. "Eaton, Purcell!" He pointed each of us to clusters of sage, picket posts to hold, and he yelled at Taylor again, "Stop— under penalty of death!" Taylor went on, and I dug myself deep into a sage bush, and Dominique crawled toward another, our wagons clattering behind us, teams bellowing and neighing, other pickets hurrying to posts.

Taylor spurred his stallion through grass, angling toward Lalooh, and she rode swiftly on her blueberry roan, still paying Taylor no mind, widening away from the three braves—who took no notice of him either—not much.

Lalooh's roan darted sideways, dropping out of sight into a dip, and Taylor raised his breechloader, and it flashed and smoked, his shoulder clutched, I heard no bang, but Nammakin, Quiltenenock and Skistymay turned his way, swinging rifles, and Taylor went down into the dip, the braves after him, and shots popped, a sputter of fire, and the rest of the Sinkiuse spread themselves out thinly, pausing well out of rifle range, perhaps seeing for themselves the truth of what Quiltenenock had already told them—we were only one company, we had no wagon gun, our most highly-prized coup swaggered from too much drink.

The Sinkiuse showed chilling discipline. No brave charged, drew fire or moved nearer Lalooh's low spot, and then a cry shattered the lull, a long-throaty whoop. Lalooh galloped suddenly up through grass, dragging Taylor behind her roan, his body twisting and bouncing in dust, his arms and legs flapping and beating against the ground.

Two armed braves appeared riding behind her, then Nammakin and Skistymay, each waving thickly-thatched scalps.

More Indians raced from behind the Sinkiuse line, braves and squaws on foot, some Cayuse and Yakama too. They waved scalping knifes, hunting and butcher knives, and they fell screaming upon Taylor, and Lalooh sat upon her roan, straightening herself in her sage dress, her hands fixed coolly on her pommel as if she had settled something. A squaw leaped up, waving a blood-dripping arm, and bits of flesh and shreds of clothes sailed into the air around her, Indians kneeling, yipping, falling, rising blood-smeared, waving new pieces of hair, flesh-straps, the second arm—doing God only knew what with Taylor's privates, meting out revenge and punishment.

A rifle shook me, discharging close. Dominique's bullet whistled a lonely whine, climbing in a high arc above the grasses, and it scattered chaff many rods short, and then I heard the clink of his breech, a clunk, a quiet slide, a harder clunk, a louder clink, and more dust rose out to the left of the Sinkiuse line, two black flags at the front of the cloud—Kamiakin seemed about to close in from the north, and yet another mass of warriors roiled dust to the south.

"Blue Hawk!" called Dominique. "Cayuse!"

Our wagons stood unmoving down by the creek, the corral apparently ready, yet more dust roiled from the buttes behind it—Lawyer's friendlies? Looking Glass's non-treaties?

A warrior whooped from the Sinkiuse line, then another and another and another. They rode forward singly, some getting nearer, others veering off, firing at long range, probing our skirmishers.

Nammakin suddenly shrieked, coming close with other braves. He and Skistymay galloped up out of grass, and I shoved my breechloader through my bush, elevated and braced it against branches, sighted Nammakin's chin, lowered the barrel, led him, shot, and Dominique discharged too, and Narcisse's piebald whirled, its snout sprayed blood, its shoulder crumpled, and Nammakin leaped off, and the piebald dropped, its hooves kicking above the grass.

Skistymay swung his horse toward Dominique, raising his rifle, and I slid open my breech, grabbed at the spent cartridge, pulled at it, and it stuck in hot-molten lead, black-gummy powder, and I scraped it, yanked it out, Dominique hammering his gun too, knocking his breech open with a pistol-butt.

Bang! Dominique's bush thrashed, and Skistymay dismounted, drawing a revolver, and he sank in the grass, snaking around on his belly, and *Bang!* Dominique yelped. *Bang!* Dominique moaned. *Bang! Bang! Bang! Bang!* Skistymay rose, lifting a scalping knife, and I was finally loaded, and I squeezed, and *Boom!* My face throbbed, powder scorched my skin, my ears throbbed, I was blind a moment, and then the Boston rifle lay cockeyed against a branch, the breech smoking heavily, my fingers burning, and I threw myself flat, heard Skistymay chirp, grunt, Dominique's skin ripping.

I drew my pistol, starting their way, and hooves thudded close again. Lalooh galloped out in the grass, leading a second pony, and a shot banged, whistling over her head, and I saw Leggett kneel to her right, lowering his breechloader, his slouch hat poking above grass, its polka-dot band in easy range.

Bang! Nammakin fired, also kneeling in grass, his back bleeding, and Leggett dove, another gun clapped, and Lalooh flew backward, a spot of blood on the shredded-sage dress, Nicholson recoiling to her left, dropping instantly to reload. Lalooh flew through air, her mouth flying open, her wound brightening between her breasts, her eyes fixed away at Nicholson, already slitting, and Leggett fired again, and her throat spurted blood, and she sprawled into grass.

Nammakin sprang up, grabbing the extra pony, and he turned and lunged to Lalooh, and a great cry rose out in the grass, and Quiltenenock fired into the air, charging with a mass of braves, no end to their dust. The troops behind Leggett unleashed a volley, covering him, and he spun, his face a pale sheet of fear, an effective order to his skirmishers: *Fall back!*

I scuttled back beneath my bush, and Skistymay burst past, chasing Leggett, and Nammakin rose alone, mounting his new pony, wrenching his big-nosed face, his tremendous teeth. He galloped after Nicholson, whirling an axe-head on a rope, Nicholson running for his life, his men making for the wagons, and I glanced at Dominique, but I could do nothing there.

A squad of Indians pounded toward Lalooh's grass-spot, split around it, closed ranks again, and I lay squeezed beneath the lowest branches, clutching my pistol beside my head, mercy if I needed it.

Stones and dirt-clods pelted the sage, the ground shook, pom-poms pounded, leggings and war vests banged past, warriors screamed, and the air exploded with reports, braves shooting at the wagons, troops returning the fire.

A couple squaws hunched in a dust-cloud where Lalooh had fallen. They lifted her in a blanket onto her blueberry roan as two tall-painted braves watched from mounts, holding rifles cocked. The squaws cinched the blanket, keening, weeping, and they rode away up the grass with the two braves, the body jostling like a dead log against the roan.

I checked my chambers and crawled out on Nicholson's side, the gunfire continuing by the wagons, the Indians holding their siege, galloping in measured charges, shooting two or three shots at once.

I crouched up, saw Nicholson's path through the grass, Nammakin's, and I ran their way, and the black flags waved out across the grass, and I dove down. It seemed neither Kamiakin nor his warriors had advanced yet. I got up. I ran again. I glimpsed the flags and the Yakama unmoving again. I dove again, and no one fired, and I listened—expected heckling, taunting, the charge of Yakama braves, firing—heard guns back by the wagons—thought Lalooh still alive, the Yakama waiting to see her before they came en masse.

I inched my head up through seed-heads and peered the other way— the Cayuse also seemed to wait at the last place I had seen them, and I wondered if Blue Hawk and Kamiakin were refusing to fight just as they had refused to council, and they were merely watching things distantly, witnessing *Quiltenenock's* battle.

I wondered if I could raise a white flag and ask to see Lalooh—no, she was dead. As dead as the Dry Creek squaws. As dead as Dominique.

A din roared up-creek at the south end of the wagons—wood cracking and smashing, steel clanging, stock screaming, guns firing a new fury.

Braves swarmed up sideboards and slashed wagon-canvas, threw spears and shot arrows over wagons, and Skistymay lay atop a bonnet, his eagle plumes streaming, his rifle discharging into the corral, and our horses leaped out, clearing wheels, squealing, and they fled with picket-pins flying in dust, more braves riding after them, firing into the air.

Warriors waved stolen blankets, stampeding horses up-creek, and a bugler played retreat down-creek, and I slid myself down a decline, and I ran low in a ditch, and then a gulch opened, a white-dirt ravine, and I jumped over a body, and it looked like Farveaux sliced open from his chin to his navel. And another body was flung into a thorn-bush, Nicholson, his face skinless, his head a bloody pulp, and then Galloway lay doubled-over, Galloway from Kentucky who played spoons, his back checkered with bullet-holes.

The ravine dropped and turned toward hoof-beats, gunfire, and an Indian lay cheek-down. Blood poured from both sides of his breechclout as if a bullet had passed through his buttocks. A stray arrow had struck his shoulder, was stuck in past the point. The Indian held Nicholson's red beard against the ground. He raised a glazed eye as I passed him—Nammakin—he was dying too—another Boston rifle with a blackened breech lay past him—another defective rifle from Leggett, this one probably Nicholson's.

A blast boomed, and I threw myself sideways, falling against a bank, and war ponies leaped above me, braves whipping quirts, high-tailing it, and I thought an ammunition mule had blown up, and Quiltenenock was leading an orgy of celebration.

I was still intact, un-hit. I raced down the ravine, stopped, dug with my hands into dirt and stone, commenced a hole to crawl into.

The hoof-beats went on, the bank rumbled, the hole caved in, and I got up and ran around bends and down into dust and smoke, willows thick, and I knelt to take stock, and the creek hissed and gurgled, and something was rubbing against stems, leaves were dropping. Another body was laying flat on the ground near the bank, a white man. He slid slowly backward, propping his shoulders against beat-down bushes, letting his legs lie slack across a little gulley. The governor. His hands reached into his trousers, grabbed for his hernia belt, tried to pull it.

His hazel eyes lit at me through the brush, and another blast boomed, two at once. Now the shells whistled, and the explosions popped clearly. Wells was here, and Quiltenenock was fleeing from his artillery.

The governor looked toward the cannon booms, and he gave me a beseeching glance, flinching, and I pushed through the willow, slid my hands beneath him, knelt up with him, and he gasped painfully, his muscles rippling rock-hard, no bleeding anywhere.

"Eaton!" he said. "Bear up! You're crying!"

The bank gave way, and I fell clutching him, rock banging my knees, water splashing my thighs. He heaved beneath me, trying to raise his mouth from the current. He flailed his useless leg, pushing up against me, and his mouth flew open, spitting.

"Over there!" he ordered, slapping the water, pointing at the opposite bank. "Leave me! I'm all right! Get to Wells! Don't let up! Go after the hostiles!"

I had my hands on his shoulders, my knees deep in his stomach.

"The Indians defy the law, Eaton!" he said. "They defy all humanity!"

"No," I said, "you are not all right," and I shoved my palms against his brow and pushed his face back under. He grimaced desperately beneath a gliding current, his face swelling and contorting. He bucked and squirmed, but I had him pinned, and I pressed down, looking away, and Lalooh pushed down through me. Nammakin, Dominique, Narcisse, Weshanaberts, Macis, Almcotty and Sidalia pushed down through me. The Dry Creek Indians pushed down against him. Donaldson, Phelps, the slump-shouldered squaw, Long Elk, Panther, the squaw at the pine camp, the mother begging in the Grande Ronde, her children, the buffalo-robe boys, the armless squaw, the old man in the sulfur cloud, the hunchback in camas blooms, all the others pushed down, and I let go, and his body floated up, barely breaking surface.

It moved down-creek, scraping and then stopping against rock.

"No, no, no, you are not all right!" I shouted.

Willow leaves collected against the body and dammed themselves against the head and spine and legs, pooling yellow in a powder smoke hanging blue and hazy.

"You will never be all right!" I shouted.

I turned from him. I stepped out of the smoke and the creek. I started my way to report to Wells.

Acknowledgements

Though *First Territory* occurs in the Pacific Northwest, an Ojibwa man in Minnesota provided its first germ of creation. He called me off the road as I bicycled west across White Earth Reservation thirty-five years ago. He showed me his old-time rice mill, explaining how his people had harvested wild rice for centuries. Gray-haired and bespectacled, he spoke quietly, lamenting how the Dawes Act had allowed whites to buy back most of his reservation. He painted word-pictures of landscapes I would travel to, and he insisted I revisit him. He gave me my first firsthand lesson of Native history and hospitality.

Ten days later a sixty-two-year-old Assiniboine woman called me into the lee of a boarded-up store on the wind-beaten Fort Peck Reservation, eastern Montana. "The whites own most of the land here, that's the problem," she said. "But I don't trust my own people. No one follows the old ways. There's discrimination against the Indians here."

Iron bars blocked the windows and door of the town's cafe, which was entered only via the post office next door. "Look at this town," said the white owner. "It took the Indians two years to tear down what it took the whites sixty to build."

He warned me to avoid Wolf Point, but I camped at a wayside there with two Indian teenagers who worked a concession booth at the Red Bottom Celebration Grounds. The young men disdained tribal rituals. "Taking an hour to drop a feather," said one. "To pray to have patience with the white man who has always robbed them," grumbled the other.

On the Fork Belknap Reservation I hesitated at a railroad crossing blocked by heavy construction, and a tall brawny Indian smiled beneath his hard hat and easily lifted my loaded-down bike across barriers. Another Indian two-heads taller than me, a Blackfoot, addressed my anxiety about crossing the Rocky

Mountains. "Don't complain about the heat," he said. "Don't complain about the wind. And *don't* sleep in Browning." Indeed the hardware store in Browning sold no nut and bolt for my rattling bicycle but displayed numerous cases of pistols, rifles, ammunition.

Weeks later, a Franciscan nun and I watched Indians reef-netting on Puget Sound. "It is not an efficient way to catch fish," she said. "I think most of them do it only for meditative purposes."

In British Columbia I stopped to watch dip-netting on the Fraser River, and Indians shouted me away angrily. I gained understanding to their objections when I read *Bury My Heart at Wounded Knee* by Dee Brown that winter.

A few years later I visited *Pishpishaston* in Yakama and Sinkiuse country, salmon runs near Wenatchee, Washington. "This is beyond question the greatest fishery I have ever seen," said Colonel George Wright in 1856. "I have consented for those Indians to remain here and fish, and later move on to Yakima."

A.J. Splawn described Wright's efforts to contain Indians in *Ka-mi-akin: the last hero of the Yakimas*. Splawn's memoir instigated the writing of *First Territory*, but not until I had bicycled across reservations during twenty-five more years.

Other sources of *First Territory* include Teresa "Ana-hoo-ey" Kurtzhall, Virginia Beavert, www.yakamanation-nsn.gov/, Martindale's Language and Translation Center, Tamástslikt Cultural Center, Darby C. Stapp, L.V. McWhorter, Kent D. Richards, Hazard Stevens, Richard Scheuerman, Michael O. Finley, Donald M. Hines, Eugene S. Hunn, Cyrus Townsend Brady, Jeremy Agnew, Carl P. Schlicke, Robert H. Ruby, John A. Brown, Corporal E.A. Bode, Richard H. Post, Andrew Dominique Pambrun, Phillip H. Sheridan, Theodore Stern, Robert C. Carriker, Cornelius M. Buckley S.J., Edward J. Kowrach, Robert Ignatius Burns S.J., Stephen Dow Beckham, Terrence O'Donnell, Joel Palmer, Herman Francis Reinhart, William G. Robbins, Melville Jacobs, Elizabeth Jacobs, William Seaburg, Roberta Hall, Don Allen Hall, Israel S.P. Lord, Nathan Douthit, Cecil P. Dryden, Katharine P. Judson, Clifford Merrill Drury, Matilda J. Sager Delaney, Lieutenant Lawrence Kip, Reverend A.M.A Blanchet, Robert H. Utley, Major-General O.O. Howard, Helen Addison Howard, Major G.O. Haller, David Fridtjof Halaas and Andrew E. Masich.

The Official History of the Washington National Guard, Volume 2, Washington Territorial Militia in the Indian Wars of 1855-56 digitized by the Washington National Guard Historical Society also helped immensely. I will never forget Angel Sobotta, Nez Perce storyteller, advocating for indigenous languages during a campfire program at Lolo National Forest. Winona Public Library supplied numerous interlibrary loans.

Robert Olen Butler tutored me in the art of fiction outside academia, enabling me to smell sage and juniper in desert air while I searched for stories.

Special thanks to Barbi who saw glitter at every desert trickle and mountain stream.

www.ingramcontent.com/pod-product-compliance
Lightning Source LLC
Chambersburg PA
CBHW032122020726
47494CB00007BA/2197